"Da... ...ing. And I hate it."

Colin ma... ...ing and took her in ...uggestions to make. So he went to her ...instead.

She stood rigidly in his embrace. It occurred to him that he'd never known a woman as complex as Alex, as difficult to reach. She was fighting so many battles. She had to be exhausted trying to do it all on her own.

"Alex...let somebody help now and then. Maybe even somebody like me."

"What can you do for me, Colin?" she whispered against his chest. "How can you help me?"

"I don't know," he answered honestly. "Maybe just by being around."

"That's not the kind of rescue you're accustomed to. And I keep telling you...I don't *want* to be rescued."

ABOUT THE AUTHOR

The Rescuer is the twentieth published bo... ... james. Ellen won a national short-story conte... ...e was in high school, and ever since then... ...to be a writer. She's certainly succeeded! Elle... ...teresting premises, fresh, charming style and ...pealing characters have made her popular with readers the w...rld over. Bestselling author Debbie Macomber says... "I love Ellen James's stories! Her wit sparkles and he... full-speed-ahead heroines are sure to capture your heart... as they do mine."

Ellen lives in New Mexico with her husband, also a writer. They share an interest in wildlife photography and American history.

THE RESCUER
Ellen James

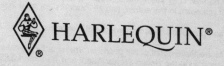

HARLEQUIN®

TORONTO • NEW YORK • LONDON
AMSTERDAM • PARIS • SYDNEY • HAMBURG
STOCKHOLM • ATHENS • TOKYO • MILAN • MADRID
PRAGUE • WARSAW • BUDAPEST • AUCKLAND

ISBN 0-373-70869-6

THE RESCUER

Copyright © 1999 by Ellen Cain.

This edition published by arrangement with Harlequin Books S.A.

Visit us at www.romance.net

Printed in U.S.A.

THE RESCUER

CHAPTER ONE

ANOTHER DAY OF SOBRIETY.

Colin McIntyre slid into his usual booth at Maggie's Diner. Less than a week back in his hometown, and already he'd fallen into the old routine. Sobriety, Idaho, was that kind of town. No wonder he'd left—and no wonder he kept asking himself why he'd returned.

Denise brought his coffee without having to be asked—straight black, no cream, no sugar.

"Pancake special this morning," she said.

"Fine," Colin told her.

She walked away, slapping a towel at the crumbs on the next table. Colin drank his coffee and looked out the window. A few summer tourists wandered along the street, pausing now and then at the redbrick storefronts. In the distance rose the mountains of the Idaho Panhandle, blanketed thickly with pine. Admittedly the view was majestic—but the whole time Colin was growing up he'd wanted to get beyond those mountains. He'd been restless. Unfortunately, when he'd finally left town at eighteen, the restlessness had followed him. It followed him still.

Now a woman came along the sidewalk, and stopped to peer up at the diner's sign. Then she opened the door, entered and glanced around.

She was very pretty, with dark blond hair falling past her shoulders, brown eyes, curves just where they should be. She wore jeans and an elegant business jacket. He liked the combination. It made her look...unpredictable.

Her gaze settled on him, and a mixture of emotions crossed her face. Wariness, reluctance... maybe even resentment? Her hand tightened on her purse and she half turned toward the door, as though to leave. He couldn't help being intrigued when she turned slowly back and stepped toward him. She seemed about to speak. But then she changed her mind and sat down in the next booth over. Denise drifted out of the kitchen and took her order: tea and the pancake special.

The woman brought a book out of her purse and started to read. Colin sipped his coffee and watched. She was making too much of an effort to appear engrossed, purposely turning one page, then another. At last she glanced up at him. Now her eyebrows drew together, as if something about him puzzled her. She'd captured his curiosity.

"Hello," he said.

"Hi," she answered, her tone a bit strained.

He could see the book was a mystery—the cover had a stylized dead body sprawled below the title. She followed the direction of his gaze and self-consciously slipped the book into her purse once more.

"Don't worry on my account," he said. "I like mysteries, too."

She almost smiled. "I picked it up at the drugstore last night, and I can't put it down. It's not how I expected to spend my time in...Sobriety." She said the name doubtfully.

"A local joke that stuck," Colin told her. "Story goes that during the silver rush in the 1870s we had thirteen saloons but only one hotel. Kept the miners happy."

She regarded him thoughtfully. "You sound like a native of this town."

He hadn't meant to sound that way. He'd moved away from Sobriety all those years ago, and he wasn't exactly back by choice.

"Let's just say I grew up here. Care to join me?" he asked.

She seemed to think it over. Finally giving a too-careless shrug, she went and slid into the seat opposite him.

"Colin McIntyre."

"Alex Robbins." They shook hands briefly.

Denise brought both orders of pancakes, doing only a slight double take when she saw Colin and the woman sitting together. She did, however, give him a meaningful stare as she put the plates before them. He'd known Denise ever since she was a kid tagging after her brother, one of Colin's high school friends.

"Thanks, Denise," he said now.

"Sure thing," she answered flippantly. She set down a cup of tea, replenished his coffee, gave him another look and went off again.

"Am I missing something?" Alex Robbins wanted to know.

"Not much," he said. "It's just that Denise figures she knows everything about me. She probably thinks I'm trying to pick you up."

"Are you?" Alex asked.

Colin poured blueberry syrup over his pancakes. "I'm out of practice when it comes to picking up women. And, as I recall, I wasn't very good at it."

She eyed him consideringly. "You're being modest, no doubt. Something tells me you don't have to try very hard when it comes to women." It didn't sound like a compliment. But she was right about at least one thing. Since his divorce, he hadn't tried very hard where women were concerned. Somehow he'd lost the knack for doing all the little things you were supposed to do to attract a woman. Any relationships he'd had could be blamed on happenstance, and they'd all been for the short term. Maybe he was just proving his ex-wife right: he was no good for the long haul.

Alex Robbins started in on her breakfast.

"No syrup?" he asked. "Trust me, it's good. Maggie's secret recipe."

She took the jar of syrup and poured out a cautious amount. "Just who is Maggie?"

"You know, of Maggie's Diner…Denise's grandmother, and founder of this place."

"Do you know everybody in this town?" Alex asked.

"Just about." He spoke without enthusiasm. "What about you?" he asked. "Vacationing in Sobriety?"

She hesitated, and again he sensed her reluctance. "Actually," she said at last, "I'm a psychologist. Mr. McIntyre, you're going to find out sooner or later. The reason I came here was…for you."

He settled back. "Hmm…I see," he said gravely. "You're here for me." He took another forkful of pancake and a sip of coffee.

Now Alex Robbins seemed impatient.

"Aren't you going to ask me what I want from you?"

"No, not really. I figure you'll tell me soon

enough. Besides, right now I'm enjoying my breakfast. I'm also enjoying sitting across the table from a pretty woman. Kind of hate to ruin the moment.''

She glanced at him sharply. "You *are* trying to pick me up.''

"Is it working?''

They gazed at each other once more. A very subtle, very appealing flush stole over her cheeks.

"Mr. McIntyre—''

"'Colin.'''

"Mr. McIntyre, I saw a video of the Bayview rescue. You were quite impressive.''

"What video?'' he asked indifferently.

She swirled the tea bag in her cup. "You're being deliberately obtuse. You must know your rescue of that child made the national news. And so, of course, did you. Not that you were cooperative about giving an interview.''

"Never did care for journalists.'' He'd finished his pancakes. Denise promptly appeared and placed a fresh stack in front of him.

"You're having more?'' Alex asked disbelievingly.

"Pancake special is all you can eat,'' Denise supplied. "And Colin has a healthy appetite.''

"Thanks, Denise,'' Colin said pointedly.

"Oh, you want me to *leave*." With a sarcastic little wave, Denise went off to another table.

"Let me guess," Alex said. "Ex-girlfriend."

"No. Denise was too smart to ever get involved with me."

Alex appeared to give this some thought. "Anyway," she went on in a determined voice, "a colleague of mine recorded you on the news and sent the video to me. She thought you'd be an excellent candidate for a study I'm conducting. I believe she's right."

Colin poured more blueberry syrup. "You know," he said, "someday I'll have to ask Maggie exactly what's in this stuff."

"Mr. McIntyre—Colin. Ignoring me won't make me go away."

"I'm not ignoring you," he said, his gaze lingering on her. He liked the way the flush deepened in her cheeks.

"Now, here's the deal," she muttered. She leaned toward him, her brown eyes serious, intent. "I'm doing an in-depth study of the Type R male. Rescuers—men who risk their lives for others. And after I saw you on that video…well, the rest is simple. When I called your number in California, your boss told me you were visiting out here—and I got on a plane from Chicago as soon as I could."

Too bad Alex Robbins wasn't just a pretty girl

in a diner. "So you want me to be a kind of guinea pig," he said.

"That's a crude way of putting it. I just want to find out what motivates someone like you, what makes you choose a job where you risk your life for others."

Maybe he was through with the pancakes after all. He took some bills from his wallet and put them on the table. "My treat," he said.

"I can pay for my own breakfast," she objected.

He stood. "Nice talking to you, Alex."

She stared up at him. "Is this your way of telling me I won't get anything from you but a free breakfast?"

"I don't think I'd make a very good guinea pig," he remarked. "Besides, you're not sure about it yourself. You don't want to be here. This whole time you've been debating whether or not you even want to talk to me. For a shrink, you're kinda easy to read, Alex Robbins."

She looked exasperated. "I'm not giving up," she said.

"Could be fun, you not giving up."

She looked more annoyed than ever.

"See you around, Alex," he said, and then he left the diner.

"HERB—YOU HERE?" Colin's voice echoed along the mine shaft. His flashlight glimmered across the walls of gray rock, where whitish beads of moisture had formed. In another hundred years or so those beads might evolve into small crystals. Another thousand years after that and the crystals might form the beginnings of stalactites and stalagmites. Life moved slowly underground—very slowly.

"Herb," Colin called again.

"Hold on...no need to shout." Colin's grandfather came trucking along the shaft from the opposite direction, his own flashlight sending a wavering beam through the darkness. "What are you doing down here, Colin? I told you when you were a kid—these tunnels aren't safe. Heard me say anything different since?"

"If they're not safe, what are you doing here?" Colin inquired reasonably.

Herb shone his flashlight over the walls. "Difference is, I know this place inside out. I know this mine better than anyone." A quiet pride had come into his voice.

"Yeah, well...I need to talk to you. Can we get out of here?"

Now Herb shone his flashlight in Colin's eyes. "Still don't like it down here, eh?" he asked skeptically. "Even after all these years?"

Some things you just didn't forget. Colin had

only been eight the time he'd gotten lost in the mine, but he still remembered: the darkness pressing down on him, the dampness of the sharp rock walls against his frantic fingers, the wavering sound of his own voice echoing back to him. It had taken six hours for his father to find him…six long hours until he was in his dad's strong arms and felt he could breathe again. That was the most vivid image he'd kept of his father. Knowing that his dad wasn't afraid. Not of the mine—not of anything. And perhaps that was when Colin himself had vowed never to be scared of anything again.

"All right, all right," Herb grumbled now.

He led the way up the slope, and he and Colin emerged onto the side of the mountain. The pungent smell of pine surrounded them. Herb didn't bother to take off his battered old miner's hat. It was probably the same one he'd worn as a sixteen-year-old, when he'd first started working underground. But now the mine was played out, abandoned. And Herb was a long way past sixteen. The deep grooves etched into his face reminded Colin of the mine walls, scarred by the years but ever enduring.

Herb looked Colin over. Colin knew that expression. The whole time he'd been growing up he'd had the feeling he was on probation with his grandfather—Herb waiting to see how he turned out before giving the okay. Colin was almost thirty-eight, but he still felt he was waiting for Herb to pass final judgment. It made for a certain restraint between the two of them. Maybe that was why he called the old man "Herb" instead of the more relaxed "Herbie" everyone else had adopted.

"I have a lot to do," Herb said, going to his truck and rummaging through the rusted toolbox in back.

Colin had been trying to pin his grandfather down these past few days, but somehow Herb always managed to avoid a serious conversation. Maybe now that they were stuck on this mountain together, Herb would have to talk.

"Lillian's worried about you," Colin said.

"What's she got to do with anything?"

"Knock it off, Herb," Colin said mildly. "I know you and Lillian are seeing each other."

Herb shrugged. "She's the one who wants to keep it a secret. She thinks it'd be a big scandal, a fifty-nine-year-old youngster like her having a fling with the seventy-six-year-old mayor of Sobriety."

Colin knew that Herb didn't mind mentioning his age because he was still fit enough to scramble through mine tunnels—and obviously still fit enough to have a fling.

"Okay, she wants it to be a secret," Colin said.

"Which means she must have been pretty upset to call me long-distance and spill the beans about being your girlfriend. Not that I have the story straight yet. Lillian's been a little obscure. Something about you running around town at midnight in a sheet—"

Herb chuckled. "Hell, if you want to know what happened, why don't you just come right out and ask? Lillian and I were down at the mining museum late one night, having a good time so to speak. When Rose Bradshaw almost walked in on us, I tried to make my escape like a gentleman. Is it my fault Rose caught an eyeful of me in that sheet and started spreading rumors that she'd seen a ghost? Good old Rose. Serves her right for being too vain to wear her bifocals."

A jay flapped by, making a racket as it landed in a nearby tree. Colin realized the absurdity of the conversation. "Look," he said, "it's not that night Lillian's so worried about. It's what came after…namely, your half-baked scheme to make people think the museum really *is* haunted."

"Nothing half-baked about it," Herb said self-righteously. "I planned the whole thing out. Made sure Rose had another sighting of her ghost… spread a few rumors of my own. Town's getting a kick out of it, and tourism's already up—exactly what we need. The way I see it, I'm only doing my duty as mayor. I'm supposed to encourage what's good for business, aren't I? Well, seems a ghost is good for business.''

The whole thing was ridiculous, but Colin had promised Lillian he'd have this talk with Herb. He couldn't very well stop now. "Okay, so you're having a little fun. But if it comes out you're behind the hoax, you'll be the town laughingstock, to use Lillian's term. It'll ruin your career as mayor."

"No one'll find out," Herb said confidently. "Lillian worries too much. Never thought you did, though. Are you telling me you flew all the way out from California for this?"

It was more complicated than that. Sure, Lillian's phone call had reminded him he was overdue for a visit to his grandfather. But it had also given Colin an excuse to take some time off work and get out of California for a while. The old restlessness had driven him—a dissatisfaction that came upon him every couple of years or so, telling him it was time for a change…time to raise the stakes, time to push himself and find a challenge more difficult than the last.

"Herb," Colin said now, "I thought being mayor meant a lot to you. Why mess with it?"

Herb got his stubborn look. "This town needs some stirring up. People like a ghost story. And if it's good for business, it's worth the risk. Maybe it'll even be good for morale. Things just haven't been that great around here since…'' When he fell silent Colin knew Herb probably wasn't thinking about the town anymore. No doubt he was thinking instead of the son he had lost some twenty-five years ago. Thomas McIntyre…Colin's father.

Herb gripped the side of the truck bed, staring off into the distance. The sadness and regret in his expression were unmistakable. He was thinking about his son, all right. Thomas, the Vietnam War hero who'd died tragically young in an automobile accident. Colin didn't think Herb had ever recovered from that loss. Maybe nobody in the family had.

Thomas was the real ghost haunting the Mc-Intyres.

IT COULD HIT ALEX at the most unexpected times.

Take right now, for instance. She was driving along the streets of Sobriety, Idaho, when just ahead she saw a young couple stopped in the middle of the sidewalk—the man speaking earnestly, the woman with her arms crossed, a resistant expression on her face.

They might just as well have been Alex and Jonathan. Only, Alex would have been the one talking so earnestly, Jonathan the one resisting. Their marriage had been like that throughout—Alex playing suitor to her husband's emotions, trying to draw them out. And Jonathan hoarding his feelings, as if they were some rare coinage and he a collector. Except, all along Alex had believed Jonathan needed to be close to her. If only either of them had known how to make it happen...

The sense of failure was so strong this time that she had to pull over to the curb for a moment. She sat there in her rental car, staring out the windshield. The couple on the sidewalk passed, the woman with her arms still crossed, striding just ahead of the man. Alex's mouth twisted in a wry smile. A man and a woman out of step. That was how she and Jonathan had been...always out of step.

Now, after eight years of marriage, it was almost over—the divorce almost final. Eight years gone, with nothing left but inadequacy and heartbreak. Alex felt as though there was a soreness inside her that would never heal. She'd loved Jonathan...seemingly desperately at times. And surely he'd loved her. So how was it that they'd both failed so utterly?

Alex laughed humorlessly. The irony was too painful. Dr. Alexandra Robbins, psychologist... mender of other people's emotional blights, yet totally unable to mend her own. At least she had one consolation—no one was likely to recognize her here in the northern reaches of Idaho. Unlike Chicago. After appearing on a few local talk shows last year, she'd suddenly had complete strangers coming up to her, asking for advice. What would those people say if they knew the disaster of her personal life?

She restarted the car and pulled away from the curb. These past few difficult months, one thing alone had kept her going—her research. It had given her an excuse to stay late at the office instead of going home to an empty house. It had kept her thoughts on rescuers…instead of the marriage she hadn't been able to save.

But then she'd received the video of Colin McIntyre, and suddenly her research was no longer an uncomplicated refuge from the realities of life. Every time she watched that video something disturbing happened to her. She'd see the image of flames burning orange-red on the screen, and her heart would pound uncomfortably. Then the camera would swing down, focusing on Colin's face…grim, angry, soot-covered. Alex would stare into the clear, startling blue of his eyes, and her heart would pound all the more, an unfamiliar anxiety washing over her.

It didn't make any sense at all. Why would an image on a television screen affect her that way?

Alex had learned that Colin belonged to an elite emergency services team in California, trained in mountain search-and-rescue, helicopter evac, earthquake relief—in short, just about any type of rescue required. She was convinced he'd give her study the spark of life it needed. Yet something warned her to stay away from him. Something dark and confusing, and almost frightening...

"What is it?" she whispered. "What's wrong with me?"

She hated unanswered questions. Maybe that was why, at this very minute, she was on her way to find Colin McIntyre.

After turning down another street, she parked in front of a quaint old house built of honey-colored stone, with a green-shingle roof that looked like thatch in need of mowing. Alex got out of her car and went up the walk. Learning that Colin's grandfather lived here hadn't been all that difficult after Alex discovered the citizens of Sobriety liked to chat about one another. That was why it had been so easy to find Colin at Maggie's Diner earlier today. Now she climbed the steps of the porch and lifted the old-fashioned brass knocker. After a moment the door swung open, and a shaggy white terrier came shooting out.

"Oh, hell," said a gravelly voice from inside

the house. "Grab him, will you? He knows I want to give him his medicine. Won't let me near."

An elderly man appeared at the door, and Alex obligingly scooped up the little dog. It squirmed in her arms but then peered at her curiously.

"Hey, you're adorable, aren't you?" she murmured.

"He already knows that," said the man. "Makes him think he can get away with murder."

Still cradling the dog, Alex examined the old man, who had shaggy white hair of his own. He was unmistakably Colin's grandfather—the clear, intense blue eyes were exactly the same. So, too, was the straightforward, no-nonsense manner.

"Bring him along, will you. He answers to Dusty," said Herb McIntyre, obviously not concerned about other introductions.

Alex followed him down a hall and into a spacious kitchen with porcelain sinks, checkerboard tile and an honest-to-goodness wood-burning stove.

"Sit down," said Herb.

Alex sat the dog in her lap. Herb approached with a pill in hand. Dusty buried his head stubbornly.

"Maybe you should disguise the pill," Alex said. "You know, hide it in some food."

"Tried that," said Herb. "Too smart—he

knows. Just eats around it. Now, think you can hold his mouth open while I pop it in?''

''Well...'' Alex began doubtfully.

And just then Colin McIntyre appeared. He was tall, as she'd thought, and seemed to fill the doorway. Right now he was gazing at her with something she could only call disfavor.

''So,'' he said. ''You and Herb have met.''

''Of course we have,'' said the old man. ''From the look of her, she's that pretty psychologist Denise told me about, the one you had breakfast with this morning.''

''In case you hadn't noticed,'' Colin told Alex, ''news travels fast in Sobriety.''

She nodded, unable to say anything at the moment.

''Have to get this damn medicine down somehow,'' Herb said. ''Vet's orders.''

''Maybe he just needs a little distraction,'' Colin suggested.

He pulled up a chair next to Alex. Their knees brushed as he petted the little terrier. Odd that he had such powerfully built hands, yet they could be so gentle...

Dusty was enjoying all the attention, and he relaxed enough for a pink tongue to loll out. Herb popped the pill in, and Colin held the dog's jaw

shut, forcing him to swallow. Now Dusty got an
offended look and hopped down from Alex's lap.

"Done," said Herb.

A silence descended. Herb glanced from Colin
to Alex. "Well," he said. "Guess you want me
out of here. From what Denise says, you two have
things to talk about. Come on, boy." He left the
kitchen, the little dog trotting after him.

Alex and Colin were still sitting knee to knee.
She pushed her chair back awkwardly.

"Mr. McIntyre—"

"Colin, remember?"

"Right. Colin." She felt foolish, didn't know
why, and that just made her feel more out of sorts.

He stood, took a mug from the cabinet and set
it on the table. Then he opened a tin, pulled out a
tea bag and filled a kettle with water. He placed it
on a gas oven that looked too modern next to the
lumbering wood-burning stove.

"Funny, but you don't strike me as the domestic
type," she said.

"I can boil water. Don't expect much else." He
turned his chair around and straddled it, resting his
arms along the back.

"You remembered that I drink tea," she said,
feeling more foolish than ever.

"Sometimes I'm observant," he said. "Take
right now, for instance. You've tracked me down,

Alex Robbins, but you're still wondering if you even want to talk to me.''

"Of course I want to talk to you," she said. "Why else would I be here—"

"You tell me," he said.

She stared into his eyes, and her pulse did something erratic. She reminded herself how important her research was, the one thing giving meaning and shape to her life these days.

"I've been thinking," she said, "about that phone conversation I had with your boss the other day. He said some pretty interesting things…about that apartment fire, for instance. Apparently you were more than a little reckless in the process of rescuing that little boy. So reckless that both you and your partner almost lost your lives."

She knew she was trying to goad Colin, unsettle him somehow. But all he did was gaze back at her impassively. The kettle whistled and he went to turn off the burner. After splashing some water over the tea bag in Alex's mug, he sat down again.

"Don't you wonder about it yourself?" she asked. "Why you need to risk your life."

"I do my job," he said. "That's all."

Alex shook her head. "It's never that simple."

"Guess it's not," he said. "Look at you, Alex. You keep saying you want to study me…but what

you'd really like to do is catch the next plane back
to Chicago and never see me again.''

She stared at him. ''What makes you think—''

''Like I said, Alex—I'm observant.'' He looked
at her speculatively. ''Have to admit I'm curious.
What's making you stick around here, doing something you don't want to do?''

How neatly he'd turned the conversation from
himself. Worst of all, how perceptive he was. She
didn't want to be here. She didn't want to feel this
strange unease.

''Might as well drink your tea,'' he said.

When she picked up the mug, her fingers trembled just the slightest. She set it back down
quickly. What was happening to her?

She didn't know. But whatever it was, it had
something to do with Colin McIntyre. And that
scared her most of all.

CHAPTER TWO

IF YOU WERE COMING to northern Idaho by plane, the Silver Lake airport was the closest you could get to Sobriety. Not that the airport was anything to shout about—commuter flights and twin engines were usually all that landed here. The fact that Colin's fifteen-year-old son was arriving by charter would probably cause a commotion.

Colin stood at the window of the small airport building, staring out at the tarmac. The last time he'd seen his son was a month ago, and as usual the encounter hadn't gone well. His ex-wife said he was just trying too hard with Sean, trying to make every visit an event. But when you were divorced and you only got to see your kid every so often…you had to make it an event, didn't you?

Colin had an image of the way things should be when you had a fifteen-year-old son. The teenage years were supposed to be the special years, the best time to be a dad—throwing a football around in the park, hockey games, basketball tickets to the Lakers, fishing trips and backpacking through the

Sierras. Trouble was, Sean didn't seem to like doing any of those things with his father. In fact, he didn't seem to like his father much at all.

Colin paced restlessly at the window. Sure, he'd put his time in when Sean was young. He'd done his share of diapers and midnight feedings, school plays, parent-teacher conferences. But for a while now Sean had been old enough for the good stuff—those special years. Only, the good stuff didn't seem to be good enough for Sean. What was wrong with the kid?

Of course, there'd been a new development this past year: Sean's landing a part on that TV show. It had complicated things big time. His son, the actor. He still couldn't get used to the idea. In all fairness, he knew his ex-wife couldn't get used to the idea, either. Beth hadn't gone looking to make Sean a child star. She'd just been catering a party in L.A., and Sean had been helping her out. One of the guests had turned out to be a producer. He'd been intrigued with Sean, said the boy had potential. Next thing anybody knew, Sean was reading for a part. Next thing after that, he was in a TV series. Fairy tale come true...or nightmare. Because now, according to Beth, Sean was out of control. Beth was fed up with him, and Sean was being shipped out to Idaho for Colin to "set him straight."

A speck appeared in the sky, grew larger, and soon his son's charter came in for a landing. Colin watched from the window a moment longer, then realized he should be out there with a greeting. He was halfway across the tarmac when he saw Sean emerge from the plane. Taller, it seemed, than a month ago, and a little on the lanky side. The dark glasses he had on gave him a too-sophisticated look.

Colin raised his hand. Sean didn't wave back. Instead he went down the steps and, without another glance in Colin's direction, disappeared into a limousine waiting a short distance off. Then the limo drove away.

At first Colin thought it was just a misunderstanding. He even began to jog after the car. But then he realized what a damn fool he must look like, sprinting across the tarmac and waving his arms at a rapidly vanishing limousine. This was no misunderstanding. Sean had, for all intents and purposes, ditched him.

A few moments later Colin was in his Jeep. His son had a good start on him, and by the time he reached the highway he could barely see the limo way up the road. At least it was headed toward Sobriety. Colin pressed on the gas. Eventually he was right on the limo's tail. He couldn't see inside it, though, the windows were that tinted. What did he think he was going to do next—start honking, force the limo off the road? And then give his son a big welcome hug?

He followed the limo all the way into Sobriety, staring at the tinted glass that wouldn't let him see in. And he couldn't help noting that the dark barrier between his son and him symbolized their relationship precisely.

Question was…how did he get Sean to open up to him?

IT WAS ALEX'S SECOND visit to Herbie McIntyre's house. As she used the old-fashioned brass knocker, she half expected to see Dusty the terrier come bouncing out. Instead, when the door opened, she was confronted by a teenage boy. He looked familiar, and no wonder. He was so much a younger version of Colin—the same dark hair, same intent blue eyes, maybe the same stubborn demeanor.

"Hi," the boy said with interest.

"You're late, Alex."

Colin appeared behind the boy, and Alex was struck by the fact that the two were even dressed alike—khaki shorts and a Dodgers T-shirt for the man, faded cutoffs and a Packers T-shirt for the boy.

"Thought maybe you'd decided not to come," Colin said quickly.

"Actually I'm right on time," she told him, not seeing the need for that brief amusement in Colin's eyes. Colin hadn't argued about her coming over today, but he still hadn't agreed to be her "guinea pig."

"This is my son, Sean," he said. "Sean—Dr. Alex Robbins."

The boy gave Colin a disgusted glance and wandered back inside the house. Colin gazed after him with a slight frown. It seemed that the McIntyre males were at odds.

"I didn't know you had a son," Alex said.

"Unfortunately Sean doesn't appear to know it, either," Colin said dryly.

"Anything you want to talk about?"

"Do you have kids, Alex?"

"No," she said, "but I do know a thing or two about them—"

"It wasn't an accusation." He gazed at her thoughtfully. "More like a rhetorical question."

"Could we just get started? I don't think you'll find our session too painful."

"So now it's a session," he said, his tone ironic.

He led the way to a living room that was comfortably cluttered—a newspaper scattered on the coffee table, books with well-used bindings stacked on the shelves, a colorful rag rug with a dog bone tossed in the middle. What drew Alex, though, were the family photos tucked here and there. She drifted to the mantel and examined a picture of a much-younger Herb, his arm around a woman with soft, wavy hair. Another photo showed Colin with a strikingly beautiful brunette and a little boy who had to be Sean. Still another photograph, this one taking pride of place in the very center of the mantel, showed a cocky young man in an air force uniform. Again, the McIntyre genes were unmistakable.

Colin came to stand beside her, nodding at the first picture. "Herb and my grandmother. They got divorced a long time ago, but they've managed to remain friends. She's the only person who can give him as much hell as he deserves."

Alex moved on to the next photo. "Your wife?"

"Ex. Don't know why Herb's hanging on to that one."

He didn't sound disturbed, just indifferent. Alex studied the family grouping in the photograph: the little boy in front, about five years old, holding a toy airplane, oblivious to the camera, Colin with his arm draped casually around the shoulders of the beautiful brunette. She was turned toward him, laughing as if they were in the middle of an intimate conversation.

"Were you happy?" Alex asked. "I don't mean the kind of happy that people put on for the camera. I just mean…were you happy?"

He remained impassive. "Is this part of being a guinea pig?"

She lifted her shoulders. "The personal life of the Type R man—believe me, that's worth a couple of chapters in itself. But right now…I'm asking off the record."

He gazed at the photo. "We were happy for a while, I think. At least, that's my version. Maybe Beth would tell you different. She'd probably say I was a pain in the neck because I was always on the verge of breaking my neck."

"Your boss was right, then," Alex murmured. "You *are* reckless."

He gave her a sardonic glance. "That's not the only thing that drove Beth crazy. She was very good at living in the moment, taking one day at a time. I'm always pushing ahead. Always searching for something new…something different in my life." He frowned. "Problem is, living in the moment has its drawbacks, too. If both of us had looked ahead more with Sean, we might have stopped this damned career of his before it even started."

"Sean has a career?" Alex asked, intrigued by these glimpses into Colin's life.

"Ever heard of *Arrested Development?*"

Alex nodded. "Vaguely. Television show, right?"

"I suppose," he said gruffly. "It's a sitcom about a police detective raising his two nephews. Sean plays the oldest kid."

"No wonder he's so familiar. I thought it was just the resemblance to you…but I've seen his face before. A couple of magazine interviews, maybe."

"Too many," Colin muttered. "All the publicity's gotten out of hand. Everything's gotten out of hand—Sean included."

Alex picked up the photo, examined it again, then set it down.

"Sometimes," Colin said, "I tell myself that if Beth and I were still together, Sean would be a whole lot better off."

Alex heard the regret weighting his voice. "Hey," she said, "it's not like divorce is so uncommon. Seems to be happening to everybody."

He studied her some more, and she found herself saying the rest of it. "My papers should be in the mail any day." She tried to sound flippant but didn't succeed. She was grateful when Colin didn't attempt to be sympathetic.

"Married how long?" he asked.

"Eight years, if you count our anniversary last month. Not that I'm counting." She wished she'd never brought up the subject of divorce—hers or anyone else's. And she wished Colin McIntyre wouldn't stand and stare at her with that quizzical expression.

"When the marriage turns bad," he said at last, "it's hard not to blame yourself."

She glanced away. "Oh, I'm not that noble. I blame *him* plenty, too." She went to sit on the sofa, then reached into her tote bag, drew out her tape recorder and set it on the coffee table. "We've gotten off track and we haven't even started."

"What is it we're starting, Alex?" he asked gravely.

"Face it," she said. "You're curious. You want to know what it's like to be a…guinea pig."

He managed just a hint of a smile as he sat down in the armchair across from her. His attitude was clear: he gave her research so little credence he didn't really care what she did next. Against her will, her gaze traveled over him. He looked ruggedly masculine in those shorts and T-shirt, his feet bare. Alex suddenly felt fussy and overdressed in her business suit.

She pulled a binder from her tote bag and flipped it open to the questionnaire she'd revised again and again. She started the tape recorder, then glanced at Colin.

"Will this bother you? Having their words on tape makes some people uncomfortable."

"Not me," he said.

She had the feeling that not much bothered Colin McIntyre. Of course, you couldn't afford to be bothered by much when you risked your life for a living.

"Now," she said, "the first thing I'd like to discuss—"

"Why rescuers?" he asked.

She frowned. "What do you mean?"

He settled back in his chair, looking completely at ease. "I'm just wondering why you decided to study so-called rescuers."

She tapped a pencil against her questionnaire. "Well…if you must know, I've often asked myself the same question. It's something that's compelled me for a long time now. I don't know *why* exactly." When she realized how inadequate that sounded, she went on quickly. "I just kept wondering about people who put themselves on the line for others. You could say they do it out of altruism or heroism, but it's a lot more complicated than that. I've found that a particular personality is drawn to rescue work. I've studied both men and women, of course, but I've chosen to focus on the Type R male—"

"You keep acting like I'm supposed to fit some kind of type," Colin said.

"Let's see…the Type R male. Arrogant, self-assured, thinks he's invincible, doesn't trust anybody but himself. Any of that sound familiar?"

Colin nodded. "Always wanted to be the kind who'd break the mold."

"That's another characteristic of the Type R man," Alex said. She scanned her questionnaire. "Now, first off—"

"The guy you married. Was he a Type R?"

She stared at him. "What does that have to do with anything?"

"Just curious," he said.

This interview wasn't going exactly the way Alex had planned. "No, Jonathan is not a rescuer. He's a lawyer, and a corporate one at that."

Colin looked reflective. "Thought maybe you had a personal interest in the subject."

"Right," she said sarcastically. "Like maybe I only date firemen."

Somehow she had to get this discussion back on Colin. Once more she reached into her tote bag; this time she brought out a videotape.

"How much stuff have you got in there?" he asked.

"This is all that'll be necessary. Can we play it?"

He didn't seem overjoyed at the prospect, but he popped the tape into a VCR across the room and turned on the TV. A few seconds later an image of fire and smoke flared on the screen.

Alex stiffened, but she forced herself to take a deep breath. She knew what to expect—every time she watched this video, she felt an uneasiness she couldn't explain.

Now it was starting all over again. A news anchor was talking about the small brushfire that had set an apartment complex ablaze…then the camera was panning the building itself, several stories high, smoke billowing from the windows, flames burning orange-red…

Alex felt as though a vise had clamped itself around her. The panic was worse this time—much worse. Suddenly she couldn't breathe. *Easy,* she told herself, but the word made no sense. Nothing made sense at this moment.

The camera swung down and centered on Colin's face—grim, soot-covered, eyes a cold, startling blue. And the vise tightened around Alex.

She stood, scarcely knowing she had. All she wanted to do was run away, escape the fear that engulfed her. The image of Colin's face froze on the screen. Then Colin himself came to her. He took her hands in his.

"What is it, Alex?" he asked quietly. "What's wrong?"

She couldn't answer him. All she could do was stand there, gripping his hands as if only he could save her.

But how could he save her from anything, when he was the one who frightened her?

FAMILY DINNER at the McIntyre house. Lots of good food and conversation. Amendment: lots of good food—tonight Herb had broiled some steaks and served them with crusty rolls, mashed potatoes and green beans—no conversation. The three McIntyres sat around the dining room table, no sound but the clink of forks against plates. Colin told himself you couldn't have everything.

At last Herb, pointing his fork at Sean, spoke. "You're next."

"Say what?" Sean muttered, slouching in his chair, a long-suffering expression on his face.

"Tomorrow night you make dinner," Herb told him. "And then your dad's in charge night after that. We rotate."

"Like I cook," Sean said.

"You'll learn or you'll go hungry," Herb retorted. "I guess on that television show of yours everything's catered. But we don't cater here."

Sean mumbled something.

"Sean," Colin said, "if you have something to say to your great-grandfather, say it. Otherwise…"

"I can handle him myself," Herb said testily. "And I sure as hell don't need anyone calling me a great-grandpa. Herb will do nicely."

Maybe no conversation was the better choice. Sean hadn't seen his great-grandfather—correction, Herb—since he was ten. The intervening five years hadn't contributed to family togetherness, it seemed.

Sean mumbled something else.

"Speak up," ordered Herb.

Sean glared at him. "I can't cook."

"First lesson is tomorrow."

"Hell," said Sean.

"That's enough," said Colin.

"I told you," grumbled Herb, "I can handle him myself. Kid, you really like people waiting on you all the time? That's what you want?"

Sean looked beleaguered. "I work."

"Not real work," said Herb.

"Yeah, right," said Sean in a long-suffering tone. "Too bad I'm not slaving in a mine."

"Damn right." Herb pointed his fork again. "You find out what you're really made of when you haven't seen daylight for twelve hours, and you've got a drill hammering in your ears, and the muck is clogging your nose and your eyes, and you've just found out you're pulling a double shift.''

"Your family owned the mine,'' Sean said. "You didn't have to work in it.''

"I wanted to work,'' said Herb. "I was glad to work. No catering for me.''

"Hell, I *work*—''

"Not according to your mom,'' said Herb. "According to her, lately you do everything but. Out late with a bunch of jerks.''

"They're my friends—''

"Some friends, according to your mom.''

"When the hell does she talk to *you*—''

"Take it easy, both of you,'' said Colin. "Sean, clean up your language and speak to your great— speak to Herb with a little respect. And Herb… give Sean a break. He does have a job. Maybe it's not the kind of work you're used to—but it's work.''

"Gee, thanks, Dad,'' Sean said caustically.

Colin studied his son. The boy had a belligerent attitude, but there was also a strain to his features, and an unhappiness the boy couldn't quite disguise. You shouldn't look like that at fifteen. Colin wondered what was going on with his son—and acknowledged he'd better find out soon.

"You know, Sean,'' he said, "you can kick

back a little here. This is supposed to be a vacation for all three of us.''

"Right," said Sean in a low voice. "Just the three of us. Sure."

"Sean," Colin said, "whatever trouble you're having, it might do you good to talk about it."

"Who says I'm having trouble?"

"Your mother, for one," Colin said. "Not that she'd need to—it's pretty obvious something's bothering you. I'm a good listener, believe it or not. Herb's a good listener, too, even though he'd like you to think otherwise."

"I'll listen to anything that makes sense," Herb said gruffly, tossing Dusty, who sat at his feet, a bit of crusty roll.

"I didn't want to come here," Sean said.

"You think that's a surprise?" Herb asked. "All you've done since you got here is mope. Maybe we don't have enough fans asking for your autograph."

Sean stood up. For just a second he wore an expression of pure misery. But then it was gone, replaced by the belligerence. "Hell," he said to the room at large, and made his exit.

Colin and Herb watched him go. "You could let up on him a little," Colin said.

Herb snorted. "Think your method's any better? One minute you're disciplining him, the next you're making excuses for him. I'm just trying to rile him, get him to open up. Something's bugging him big time, and he needs to let it out.''

Colin could agree on the last point. He just didn't agree with Herb's way of doing things. Of course, his way wasn't proving any better.

He didn't know how to get through to his own son.

CHAPTER THREE

MAIN STREET IN SOBRIETY, Idaho, consisted of several blocks of ornate, redbrick buildings, facing each other like proper Victorian ladies and gentlemen in an old-fashioned line dance. Alex wandered along, stopping occasionally to gaze through store windows at any number of knickknacks. She knew that when you were a tourist you took leave of your senses and bought silly refrigerator magnets, gaudy teacups and cheap sweatshirts. Of course, Alex wasn't in Sobriety as a tourist, and so far she'd managed to restrain herself.

"Hey, Dr. Alex."

The voice came from behind her, deep and easy. Colin's voice. She turned around and faced him with at least the appearance of calm.

"Hello," she said. "I'm surprised to see you, Colin. Our appointment isn't for two hours."

"Appointment...that's such an official-sounding word. How about we make it a date, instead?"

She saw the humor in his eyes and knew she ought to say something repressive. But all she could do was stand there gazing at him, in the middle of the sidewalk. Today he wore jeans and a blue-gray polo shirt. He looked dangerously handsome.

Alex still felt humiliated over what had happened yesterday, the way she'd lost control and panicked at that video. Worst of all was knowing that Colin had seen her reaction. She'd been trying to prove how strong she was, how in control…and she'd proved just the opposite.

"Had a busy day?" he asked now.

"Yes," she lied. She'd wanted to keep away from him until this evening. A little time alone, she'd told herself. Surely that was all she needed. But almost twenty-four hours had gone by since she'd last seen him and she still felt the same mixture of fascination and foreboding.

She started walking again, Colin keeping pace beside her. "I've had a very interesting day, in fact," she said. "I've learned that the big news in Sobriety is the ghost at the mining museum, but you have to be there at midnight to have any hope of seeing it."

Colin looked disgruntled. "Who's spreading the ghost stories?"

"Let's see…the lady at the drugstore." Alex didn't mention that she'd bought another mystery there. "And the man at the gas station. Oh, yes, and Denise at Maggie's Diner. She was the first person who told me about it. Apparently the ghost is a miner who died in a cave-in back in 1902."

Colin looked positively pained.

"What's the matter?" she asked. "You don't like ghost stories?"

"Depends on the ghost," he said. "So, Alex…you haven't told me whether you're going out with me tonight."

"Colin," she said firmly, "I didn't come all the way to Idaho so we could *date*."

As they walked, he took her hand in his. "Sometimes things happen that you don't expect. Like dating."

"You're just trying to get out of being part of my study," she said.

"Are you sure?"

Right now she wasn't sure of anything. Except that holding hands with the most attractive man she'd ever known was definitely not a good idea.

"Colin," she said. "I'm not officially divorced yet."

He twined his fingers through hers. "Okay, we won't call it a date. We'll just go out to dinner."

At last she had the fortitude to pull away. "You know, if you cooperated a little," she told him, "we could actually make some progress. The sooner that happens, the sooner you'll be rid of me.''

Colin took her hand again and brought her to a stop. ''What makes you think I want to get rid of you, Alex?''

She looked into his eyes and saw the humor still there. But she saw something else, something that sent a treacherous warmth all through her. When at last she wrenched her gaze from him, it did no good. Now she saw a reflection of her and Colin in a shop window. Saw the way she was leaning toward him just a bit, as if he were a magnet drawing her. She knew body language, and she knew what her body was saying now.

She pulled away from him a second time, taking a step back. ''Colin, I'm not going on a date with you. Not only am I still a married woman, but I'm a researcher. It isn't exactly ethical for a researcher to get involved with her…subject. Whether you like it or not, I *am* researching you.''

''Even researchers have to eat dinner,'' he said. ''Besides, I have a confession. Tonight my grandfather's giving Sean a cooking lesson and I'd just as soon steer clear.''

She lifted her eyebrows. ''Playing hooky?''

He appeared serious for once. ''You could say that. I've spent the past few days trying to get through to Sean, and I'm further away than when

I started. No matter what I say, he thinks it sucks. So here I am...taking a break from my own son.''

Alex gazed at Colin, and this time what she saw was a perplexed father looking for answers. That got to her more than anything.

''So, what time *is* this dinner thing of ours?'' she wanted to know.

ALEX WONDERED IF SHE'D ever seen anything so beautiful. She'd run into Colin in downtown Sobriety less than an hour ago, but already he'd whisked her away for their ''dinner.'' They were now driving in his Jeep up one of Idaho's deep green, pine-forested mountains. Far below, Silver Lake shone molten in the setting sun.

''Breathtaking,'' Alex murmured.

''Sometimes I forget what it's like up here,'' Colin said, ''and I let too much time go by without coming back.''

She glanced at him. ''You look like someone who belongs in these mountains,'' she said. ''They're ominous and gorgeous all at once.''

''Ominous...and gorgeous,'' he said in a doubtful tone. ''Is that what you think of me?''

She regretted her choice of words. She *did* think he was gorgeous, but there'd been no reason to say so.

"I wish you'd tell me where we're going," she said.

"Don't you like surprises, Alex? Me, I can't stand previews. I prefer the unexpected." He took the winding road expertly, driving a little on the fast side but always in control.

"You really are the Type R male," she told him.

"Lord, not that again."

"That's what I'm here for, remember? The Type R usually knows just how far he can go. He pushes a situation right to the edge but knows when to draw back. Of course," she said reflectively, "according to your boss, you *don't* always know."

"Alex, we're on a date, remember?"

"No date," she said. "Just dinner."

He downshifted for a curve in the road, and then the Jeep surged forward again. The road took them to the very top of the mountain.

Colin turned into a gravel parking lot and came to a stop in front of a large log building. He frowned. "What the heck...?"

"Something unexpected?" Alex asked.

"I'll say. There used to be a fancy restaurant here. The kind of place you'd bring a date to when you wanted to impress her."

They got out of the Jeep and approached the rustic building. Rock music blasted from within, and a sign over the door read simply, The Pub.

"Give me a break," Colin said.

Alex hooked her arm through his. "Lighten up. We're welcoming surprises...remember?"

"What has you in such a good mood?" he grumbled.

"Finding out that the Type R man is like the rest of us. Now and then he likes things to be predictable, too."

Colin looked disgruntled, but they went inside. The air was murky; the decor consisted of rough-hewn tables and chairs, a jukebox and a cramped bar. The place was crowded with people who appeared to have an average age of twenty-one.

Alex led the way to one of the few empty tables by the window, and she and Colin sat across from each other. The music from the loudspeakers blared right above them.

Colin got up and went to the jukebox. He dropped in a few coins, punched a few buttons. The loudspeaker cut out as the jukebox took over. Early 1960s rock replaced the 1990s variety.

Colin sat down again and picked up the menu in front of him. "The roast beef sandwich doesn't sound so bad."

"I'm starving," Alex pronounced. "I'll eat anything."

Surprisingly the food turned out to be delicious. The sandwiches were on thick, crusty bread and came with crisp onion rings and fresh alfalfa sprouts. The beer was imported and served in frosty glasses.

Colin settled back in his seat. "Want to tell me about it?" he asked.

"About what?" she murmured idly.

"About what happened yesterday at my grandfather's house. About what had you so scared."

"You really know how to ruin a good mood," she complained. "I suppose you brought me up here just so you could grill me about—"

"Hey, I'm not the shrink here. But I can tell when somebody's bothered about something." He frowned. "Take my son, for instance. I know he's unhappy. Not that I know why—since he isn't exactly forthcoming. Then again, neither are you, Alex."

She stared down at the table, running her fingers across the rough surface. She could pretend nothing was wrong or she could tell the truth. Unfortunately she didn't really know what the truth was.

"Colin," she said reluctantly at last. "I wish I understood it myself. Ever since I first saw that video…I've had a reaction that I can't explain. There's something about that fire, and something about *you*. Something disturbing, maybe even frightening." She waved a hand in frustration. "But when I try to figure out what it is…it's like fighting my way through fog. I can't *see* anything. All I have are feelings, and murky ones at that. You and I never even met until I came to Sobriety. So what is it about you and that video that makes me so uneasy?''

Colin looked thoughtful. ''If a patient came to you with this, what would you do?''

She sighed. ''I'd try to find out if the uneasiness was linked to something in the patient's past. But, Colin—that's exactly what I've been trying to do. I've been looking into my past and searching for some connection. I just don't see any! I've had such an ordinary, uneventful life.''

''Nobody's life is really uneventful,'' he remarked. ''I don't need a shrink to tell me that.''

She gave him an exasperated glance. ''Here are the facts. I grew up in Montana. My father died of heart disease when I was six years old. My mother had a difficult time afterward, but she managed to raise me single-handedly. When I was eighteen, I went off to Chicago for college. I got my degree, went to graduate school, got married…and now the divorce. That's it. I know your next question, of course. Could I be repressing some memory that gets triggered by that damn video, by *you*. Well, anything's possible, I suppose. But like I've said, my life has been ordinary. There's absolutely nothing in my background to indicate hidden traumas or such.''

Colin drank his beer. ''What would you tell a patient who said something like that?''

The man truly was aggravating. ''Oh, all right. I'd say that even the most innocent-looking life can hold secrets…but, dammit, that doesn't mean *my* life has secrets.''

He didn't answer, just gazed at her steadily. It was worse than if he'd tried to argue with her. Fortunately, her dessert arrived just then, giving her something else to focus on. Unfortunately by now she was too keyed up to enjoy the piece of peach pie as she ought.

Now she felt a sadness inside that was becoming all too familiar. She stared out the window, hoping Colin wouldn't notice.

''You might as well talk about it,'' he said.

''Just that divorce is rotten.''

''Even more rotten than a marriage gone bad?'' he asked.

She ate a bite of peach pie. ''The waste of it is what I hate most,'' she said. ''You try so hard to build something, to make it work. All those years…and then it's over. All for nothing.''

''Sort of like an investment that didn't pan out,'' Colin suggested.

Alex shook her head. ''That sounds too cold and

logical. Marriage and divorce aren't like that. They're messy and irrational…Colin, don't you wish sometimes you could just start over? Erase your mistakes as if they'd never happened?"

"Sure," he admitted. "Maybe, if I could go back, I'd realize Beth and I weren't suited for each other. Except Sean came out of the marriage. Maybe that means it wasn't such a mistake."

"Kids make a difference," Alex said, and she couldn't keep the wistfulness from her voice. "When you're getting divorced, people tell you to be grateful you don't have children. But if Jonathan and I had had a family…" She trailed off, not wanting to say the rest.

Colin, however, wouldn't let the subject go. "I take it you wanted kids, and he didn't."

"No," she said with an odd calm. "It was the other way around. He wanted children. He thought it would save the marriage. When he was feeling good, he could make it sound so wonderful…how it would be once we had a family. But I kept saying no. You see, Jonathan was becoming so moody and angry with *me*…why would he be any different with a child?" She stopped. She feared that if she said anything more, all the sorrow and pain and regret inside her would come tumbling out. And Colin, sitting there contemplatively, would see it all.

But then, to her relief, he was the one who broke the moment.

"Let's get out of here," he said.

Only a short time later, they were in the Jeep again, headlights penetrating the deep Idaho night. They drove along the mountain summit and eventually turned onto a steep dirt road. The Jeep bounced along, then came to a halt in front of a wooden fence.

"I give up," Colin said wryly. "This used to be Make-out Lane. Now there's a No Trespassing sign."

"Everything changes, I guess."

"Funny, the whole time I was growing up I couldn't wait to get out of Idaho. All I wanted was something different—something more exciting. But in the back of my mind, seems I wanted everything here to stay the same."

She could understand that. You needed a constant in your life, something you could count on somehow. "Colin...relax. I think we're having a good time almost in spite of ourselves. And maybe things haven't changed all *that* much. You're up here with a girl...."

"Not just any girl." He turned toward her.

The bucket seats of the Jeep made things awkward, but Alex found herself leaning into the curve of his arm. She stayed like that for what seemed a long moment, and it felt good...too good. Until now, she'd been able to control the way Colin made her feel. She'd managed to dismiss any stirrings of attraction, any hints of desire. But with his arm around her like this, she could no longer dismiss the craving she felt.

His fingers brushed over her cheek in a slow caress...and then another caress. She remained motionless, almost breathless, as his touch awakened all her senses. At last he tilted her face toward his.

"Colin," she whispered. He didn't answer, not in words. Instead, he brought his lips to hers.

This was no tentative first kiss, no tepid exploration. It was raw need, powerful and overwhelming. Alex felt as if she had been swept off the mountaintop. She clung to Colin, and molded herself closer to him, and opened her mouth willingly to him.

But all the while she knew what a mistake it was.

SOBRIETY'S SMALL MINING museum hardly seemed a place to be haunted. Tucked away on one of the side streets off Main, it housed a modest collection of pickaxes, shovels, water canteens, rusty pocketknives and other paraphernalia left behind by long-ago miners. It had a friendly, unimposing, somewhat dusty atmosphere. Colin figured that any self-respecting ghost would pick a more evocative locale—one of the town's old saloons, for example. If Herb wanted to stage more hauntings, he should consider that. Then again, Colin didn't intend to put any ideas in his grandfather's head.

He pushed open the door of the museum and went inside. Lillian Prescott, his grandfather's fifty-nine-year-old girlfriend, glanced up from behind the souvenir counter.

"Colin, I'm so glad you're here." She went to the door, put up the Closed sign and came back again. Lillian had an air of mystery about her, which Colin suspected she deliberately cultivated. Rumor had it that when she'd gone away to college back in the late fifties, she'd had a couple of affairs and become, in Sobriety terms, a woman of the world. That she'd returned home eventually and settled down hadn't quelled the rumors any. Every six months or so when she went off to Boise for a couple of days without telling anyone why, people liked to speculate that she was going to rendezvous with her married lover. Lillian fueled the speculation by saying nothing at all. For all Colin knew, Herb had some serious competition in Boise.

"Colin," she said now in a distressed tone, "you have to stop your grandfather. I just found out he's planning to bring a parapsychologist to town—a ghost expert.''

"He's really getting into the spirit of this thing," Colin remarked. "No pun intended."

Lillian gave him a withering glance. "You're not taking this seriously enough. I mean, he's actually advertising to get someone out here. He says somebody trying to verify the town haunting will increase its authenticity." She groaned and sank onto the stool behind the counter. "Forgive me for telling you this, Colin, but your grandfather is nuts."

"That's some way to talk about your significant other."

Lillian's expression became guarded. "Please don't get in the habit of saying that. I took you into my confidence only as a last resort."

"Why not just admit to the world that you're seeing Herb?" Colin asked. "What's so bad about it?"

"Nothing," she said, looking uncomfortable. "I just don't think the entire town needs to know about my personal life. What I do is my own business."

"Do you think people would care—"

"In this town they'd care, all right," she said. "Folks don't have enough to do, so they sit around talking about one another…and I refuse to be anybody's topic of conversation.''

Colin figured something else was at stake here, but Lillian was already changing the subject.

"You and I have more important things to discuss,'' she said. "Such as what will happen when the town finds out Herbie is bringing in an expert to document his *bogus* ghost.''

It was an interesting twist, Colin had to admit. "Okay, I'll try talking to him again. But you know what my chances are.''

Now Lillian looked worried. "Somebody's got to stop him before it's too late. He'll ruin everything—his reputation, his political career…''

Colin didn't think being mayor of Sobriety qualified as a political career, but he didn't want to tamper with Lillian's illusions.

"What's he doing it for?'' she went on. "All this nonsense about a ghost being good for the town—I don't buy that for a second.''

"Maybe he just wants to prove he can shake up the place,'' Colin said. "Nobody else has tried that in a long time.''

"Nobody but your father. All those years ago… he was a bit wild, Colin, but so talented. So full of life and energy and charm. The way everyone used to turn out for those high school basketball games just because your dad was playing.''

Colin had long since grown accustomed to how people in Sobriety spoke of his father. They always had some story about Thomas McIntyre…high school basketball star, war hero, town golden boy. But none of the stories ever seemed quite real to Colin. They were too much the stuff of legend, too easily recounted, as if people had forgotten about the flesh-and-blood Thomas behind the glorious achievements. Colin had been ten when his father died, old enough to have memories of his own, yet he'd heard the stories so many times they'd taken over.

Lillian was rearranging the pieces of quartz and silver ore on display behind the glass counter. "Something's just occurred to me," she said. "What we really need is a psychologist—not a *para*psychologist. What about that shrink of yours, Colin? Is she trustworthy?"

Colin observed Lillian dourly. "Who says I have a shrink?"

"For crying out loud," Lillian said, "have you forgotten what this town is like? Everyone knows you took her out to dinner last night. Ben Morris saw you at The Pub, and you know what a gossip *he* is. Why else do you figure I have to work so hard to keep my life private?"

Colin thought about last evening with Alex. He'd been thinking about it a lot…how it had felt to hold her in his arms those few moments. He'd wanted to go on holding her, but for her that hadn't been an option. He'd never known anyone who tried so hard to stay in control. The soon-to-be ex-husband must have really damaged her somehow. Or maybe something else was to blame.

"Colin," said Lillian, "I'm just asking if this Dr. Alex Robbins is discreet."

"She's not about to go gossiping with Ben Morris."

"You don't need to tell her any details about *me,* Colin. Just ask her to talk to your grandpa. Ask her to set him straight about this ghost nonsense."

"Psychologists aren't like auto mechanics," Colin said. "They can't just schedule an appointment to fix somebody's transmission."

"Well, we'd better do something, or we'll have a *para*psychologist on our hands. Is that what you want?"

He didn't know what he wanted, it seemed. In the past, when he'd started to feel the old restlessness, he'd simply moved on, changed his life. But now things were more complicated. He had a grandfather who wasn't getting any younger. And he had a son who'd grown up too quickly. Colin couldn't just walk away from all that.

CHAPTER FOUR

THAT EVENING, ALEX SHOWED up at the McIntyre house with a sackful of groceries. She was breathless, and her cheeks were becomingly flushed again. As she shifted the bag from one arm to another, she gazed at Colin almost defensively.

"Okay, so maybe I've gone too far," she said. "But when you called and invited me over for dinner...then said it was your turn to cook so you were sending out for pizza...well, I couldn't resist taking matters into my own hands."

He leaned against the doorjamb, appreciating the sight of her. She was wearing something sleeveless, her blond hair falling over her shoulders.

The flush in her cheeks deepened. "Kissing you was a big mistake," she muttered. "So if you're thinking about last night, please stop."

"I'm thinking about right now."

"Dammit, Colin. Just...don't."

He took the groceries from her but remained on the porch. "Are you here to give me a cooking lesson?"

"Not exactly. I'm hardly the domestic type myself. But a family dinner calls for *something*."

Lettuce was poking out of the bag, and he caught the pleasing aroma of ripened tomatoes. When he went to the grocery store, he usually confined himself to microwavable selections.

"Too bad we have to make it a family dinner," he said.

She gave him a keen glance. "We already tried the one-on-one thing, and it didn't work out."

"I thought it worked out fine."

She stared at him, her eyes a very deep brown. "I know you don't take me seriously, Colin, but you could at least try." She gazed at him a moment longer. Then she took the grocery bag back from him and strode into the house.

Colin followed her down the hall to the kitchen. The material of her dress swirled invitingly against her legs as she walked and her hair rippled gold. She appeared soft and feminine, but he sensed an implacable core. She gave the impression that she'd been taking care of herself for a very long while and she didn't want any help with the job.

When she reached the kitchen, she started removing items from the bag and placing them on the counter: the lettuce and tomatoes, two packages of whole wheat hamburger buns, a jar of pickles, a jar of relish, a bottle of ketchup, some mustard.

"Guess you didn't trust us to have any condiments," he said.

She produced a carton of ice cream and placed it in the freezer. "Got any pans?"

He had to rummage in a few cupboards before he found them.

Alex shook her head. "You really *don't* cook, do you?"

"Hey, it's my grandfather's house, not mine."

She handed him a can of peas and pearl onions. "Think you can manage that?"

Colin got busy with the opener. He found that he liked spending time with Alex in a kitchen. She didn't seem to need useless conversation. A companionable silence settled between them as he opened a few more cans and dinner began to cook on the stove.

Herb poked his nose into the room. "Hello, Dr. Alex."

"Hello, Mr. McIntyre."

"No need to be so formal," he said gruffly, "considering my grandson's finagled you into doing his work tonight."

She smiled. "Mind if I call you 'Herbie'?"

"A lot of folks do." He peered at a pan sizzling on the stove. "Those hamburgers?" he asked doubtfully.

"Veggie burgers."

"Veggie burgers?" he repeated. "Serves Colin right—he's strictly a meat-and-potatoes man." Chuckling, Herb disappeared.

"Don't listen to him," Colin said. "He's the one who thinks you can't have a meal without steak."

"You wish we were having real hamburgers, don't you?"

Those veggie things did look kind of odd, but he wasn't about to say so. Now Sean appeared, hovering uncertainly in the doorway.

"Hi," Alex said casually. "Mind doing the salad?"

He hesitated, but then he came over to the counter and confronted the lettuce. After a moment he started tearing off big pieces and tossed them into a bowl. Alex didn't comment, just went on about her business. Colin realized she was handling everything just right. She wasn't making a big deal about Sean helping out, wasn't telling him how to do things differently, wasn't paying much attention at all. Colin himself probably wouldn't have been able to resist setting the kid straight.

A short time later the four of them sat down together. Make that five for dinner, if you included Dusty. Except this time the little terrier abandoned Herb and waited at attention next to Alex's feet. The others seemed to be at attention, too. Sean

didn't slouch quite so much in his chair; Herb
didn't use his silverware to point. The food looked
all right: ravioli in tomato sauce, two different
kinds of vegetables, the haphazard salad Sean had
made. And, of course, the veggie burgers.

The conversation was actually civil. Maybe Sean
didn't contribute much, but Herb and Alex had
plenty to talk about: her practice in Chicago, his
days in the mine. It took Colin a while to realize
that he was almost as silent as his son. Apparently
he didn't have much to contribute, either.

Alex brought out the ice cream for dessert—
double chocolate chunk fudge—and the four of
them polished it off in no time. Afterward they
removed to the living room, Dusty trotting behind.
Sean hunched in an armchair, looking supremely
bored. Colin noted, however, that he didn't make
a quick exit the way he did most evenings.

Just as before, Alex gravitated to the photographs scattered around the room. No doubt she
was trying to discern the family background of the
Type R male. She picked up a photo of Colin's
parents.

Herb came over to her. "My son, Thomas, and
his wife, Jessie. Guess Colin's told you all about
Thomas."

"No," Alex said. "Actually he hasn't."

Herb glanced at Colin disapprovingly. "Thomas

fought in Vietnam. Pilot, decorated for bravery. Irony was that he made it through all that...and then he died in a car crash. He was only thirty years old.''

"I'm sorry," Alex said.

Herb nodded. Even now, over twenty-five years since his son's death, the pain was etched into his face. "Worst moment of my life," he said in a low voice. "Worst moment for all of us. I've never stopped wishing him back."

The phrases were timeworn, but they always gave Herb comfort. Some people refused to speak about their dead loved ones. Not Herb. He talked about Thomas as if somehow, someday, the words would conjure his son back.

Now he took the photograph from Alex and examined it as if he hadn't already seen it countless times. "Jessie...Colin's mom. Nice girl—even if she was a little meek for somebody like Thomas. Surprised us all, though. After he died, she remarried."

Colin had to restrain himself from speaking. Herb made it sound like she'd run out three weeks after the funeral and got herself hitched. She hadn't remarried until five years later.

"Can't understand why she picked somebody like Mack Pearson. No comparison to Thomas," Herb said.

Colin couldn't let his grandfather get away with any more. "Nothing wrong with Mack."

Herb was about to argue, but Alex intervened. "Does your mom still live in Sobriety?" she asked Colin.

"No. I left town when I was eighteen. She and Mack left the year after that. They settled in Tacoma."

"Pearson sells cars," Herb said disparagingly.

He didn't mention that Mack owned the dealership. And he never seemed to realize that his own son might have ended up doing something as ordinary as selling cars...if he'd lived. Thomas was forever frozen in time as someone young and bright and courageous. An image impossible to dim.

Alex moved around the room. She picked up another photo, got Herb on the more neutral subject of his ex-wife. She was handling the McIntyre men very adeptly, it seemed. Even Sean was still there, hunched in his chair. Maybe he was no more animated than a stump, but his presence made for a refreshing change.

So why didn't inviting Alex for a McIntyre family dinner seem like such a good idea after all?

ALEX SLEPT FITFULLY that night. Every few hours or so, she awoke feeling groggy and out of sorts.

She couldn't say why she felt so restless. She'd actually enjoyed her evening. Having Colin's grandfather and son around had lessened her awareness of Colin. Hadn't eliminated it—she'd still been uncomfortably aware of his gaze upon her—but with his family there, he hadn't been able to flirt with her shamelessly the way he usually did.

At last Alex fell into a deep, exhausted sleep. And then she dreamed. Flames surged up around her, eerily orange-red. Not the flames she'd seen on the video screen—no, flames right *here* in the room. They trapped her, licking at the edges of the bed. She couldn't move. The smoke choked her lungs, and she had to gasp for air. She was frightened. So very frightened. She began to weep.

She woke up with a start, her skin clammy, her pulse racing. The dream had been so real that she glanced around wildly, half expecting to see fire engulfing her. But there was only darkness and the cool nighttime air coming through the open window. Alex pressed a hand to her face. The tears she'd wept in the dream had felt real, too, but her cheeks were dry. It had only been a dream.

"A nightmare," Alex whispered. She reached over and switched on the lamp. She'd stayed at this small bed-and-breakfast only a few days, yet already the room's details were comfortingly familiar: the wicker dressing table with the ruffled skirt, the pine whatnot cabinet, wallpaper in a pattern of violet sprigs. The decor was too consciously quaint for Alex's taste, but right now she welcomed the cozy frilliness that surrounded her.

She realized that she was shivering. Slipping into her robe, she went to the window and shut it. Then she did something she often advised her patients to do. She took her notepad, flipped to a blank page and began jotting down everything she could remember about the nightmare. Her fingers trembled alarmingly, but she pushed on. At last she set aside the notepad, pulled up the blanket and eased her head back against the pillow. She did something else she recommended to her patients: took some deep, slow breaths. Then she turned off the light, closed her eyes and ordered herself back to sleep.

But her body refused to cooperate. Her muscles seemed tense, her thoughts scurrying restlessly. She twisted and turned, then tried to lie still again. Nothing helped.

And at last she realized that she was afraid to sleep...afraid to dream....

IN THE MORNING, ALEX FELT rotten. It wasn't just the tiredness—it was the lingering effects of that nightmare. Where had it come from? She'd never been in a fire. Not that she knew of, anyway.

Shivering anew, Alex went into the adjoining bathroom and took a long, hot shower. She emerged feeling just slightly better. When she went downstairs for breakfast, she hoped fervently that she wouldn't have to speak to anyone. Only a few other guests were staying in this place, after all. At first she thought she was in luck—there was no one else at all in the dining room. But then the owner of the house appeared.

Tina Scott was what you'd have to call a stunning redhead. No other term would do. She was probably well into her thirties, but she was one of those women who just got more beautiful with time. She wore her hair so short it stuck up in places, yet that only highlighted her noteworthy bone structure. Now, when Alex just wanted to lay her head down on the table, Tina came into the room all fresh and dewy-skinned.

"Good morning," she said, lifting the lid on one of the warming dishes. "I made sausage and eggs today, but I haven't had a chance to try them. Mind if I join you?"

Maybe Alex should have gone to the diner; at least Denise wasn't cheerful this early in the day.

Tina didn't wait for an answer. She heaped two plates with sausage and scrambled eggs, placed one in front of Alex and sat down with the other.

"Well," she said, "how's it going with my hunk of an ex-boyfriend Colin McIntyre?"

It was a question calculated to stir interest. Alex prodded her eggs with the fork. "This is the first time you've mentioned a connection with him," she said guardedly.

"Connection...that's what it was, all right. Oh, *he* probably wouldn't call it that. When he was in college he came back to town every year on vacation and swept me off my feet, and then he'd leave again. A summer romance—five summers in the making."

Tina sounded caustic. And Alex, despite herself, was downright curious. "Seems both you and Colin have moved on," she said as neutrally as possible.

"He moved on first, honey." Tina propped her chin in her hand. "Let's face it," she said matter-of-factly. "I've always had guys swarming around. I'm not being conceited or vain. That's just the way it is. I attract men, all right? Even in this Podunk town, which is why I've never bothered leaving. But you get too much of a commodity and it starts to lose its value. Know what I mean? In the end, a girl wants quality, not quantity. And Colin...he's definitely quality. Don't you agree?"

Alex didn't have an answer. All she could think about was the fact that beautiful women attached themselves to Colin. She'd seen that photograph of his ex-wife, and Beth was as much a showstopper as Tina Scott. None of this stirred Alex's confidence, especially the way she felt right now—tired, dreary, her eyes scratchy.

She had to remind herself she was not one of Colin McIntyre's *women*. And meanwhile Tina was gazing at her expectantly.

"As long as you're being frank," Alex said, "might as well spill everything. You want something from me, don't you? Can't imagine what, though."

Tina smiled, and was more dazzling than ever. "Honey, it should be perfectly easy to guess. I want you to help me get Colin back!"

BY LATE AFTERNOON, Alex had sat through a double feature at The Sunshine, Sobriety's one movie theater. She hadn't frittered away her time at the movies in the middle of the day like this in ages. She'd come to Idaho with such a sense of purpose, determined to plow ahead with her research. Now she felt like a train that had derailed, and she couldn't even say why.

Grouchily she emerged from the theater, squinting a little, wondering why anyone would name a place where you had to sit planted in the dark for several hours The Sunshine. And there, big as life, was Colin McIntyre, waiting for her. He was wearing shorts again, with a T-shirt and sandals, and he was better-looking than any of the movie actors she'd seen on the screen. More masculine, more vibrant. More everything.

"How did you know I was here?" she asked.

"Lucky guess. Denise hasn't seen you at the diner, you haven't been hanging out at the mining museum...not too much other entertainment in Sobriety."

She started walking. He kept pace.

"Explain something to me, Colin," she said. "You don't really want to get involved in my research, but you keep turning up to look for me. Does that make any sense?"

"In a convoluted way—yes," he said agreeably. "I'll tell you all about it. Just as soon as you tell me what's bugging you."

"Nothing," she muttered.

"It's getting worse. Whatever's bothering you... it's definitely worse."

She stopped, holding her arms tightly across her chest. "What makes you think that?"

"I keep telling you, Alex. I'm observant."

If only he would go away and leave her in peace. Instead he led her to one of the benches that fronted Main Street. It was fashioned elaborately of wrought iron and weathered planks, and it looked like the kind of bench old-timers would lounge on to watch passersby. Colin prodded Alex down beside him.

"I feel ridiculous," she said.

"Always helps to talk about things."

"You act like you're—like you're trying to rescue me," she burst out. "But I'm not like one of the people in that apartment fire, Colin. I don't need saving."

He just looked at her, and at last she let out a shaky breath.

"All right," she said. "Last night I had a nightmare. It was about fire. I was right in the middle of it. There was smoke in my lungs, and I couldn't breathe. I couldn't move..." If secretly she'd hoped uttering the words would bring relief, she was wrong. That damn nightmare had been haunting her all day, and it still wouldn't let her go.

Colin waited, as if knowing she needed to say more. She gave a bleak laugh.

"You know what bothers me the most? In the dream—the nightmare—I didn't do anything to save myself. I just watched the flames and...I cried. I acted so helpless."

"I can see why that would bother you," he remarked. "You're the least helpless woman I know."

She looked at him closely, but today she didn't

see any humor in his eyes. "You really believe that?"

"You might as well be wearing a sign—No Rescuers Allowed."

A little of the tension left her, and she lifted her face to the warmth of the afternoon. The sky was a pure china-blue, unlike any she'd seen in Chicago. In fact, she knew of only one other place that had a sky like that. Montana.

She straightened. It had been years since she'd been back to Montana. Why think about home now?

Colin stretched out his legs and propped his arm on the back of the bench as if he meant to stay a while.

"Don't you have anything better to do?" she asked.

"I'm trying to figure out when you might have been in a fire."

She felt a chill deep inside. "It was a nightmare, that's all. Inspired by that video of the apartment fire, I'm sure."

He wouldn't relent. "So why does the video disturb you?"

She clenched her hands. "I don't know! But think about it, Colin. If I *had* been in a fire, don't you think I'd remember?"

"What's that word you psychologists use? Repression…"

"Dammit, even if I'd *repressed* the memory, wouldn't somebody have told me about a fire?" she demanded. "Somebody like my own mother?"

"You could always ask her."

She stared straight ahead, silent for several moments.

"You don't understand," she told him last. "My mother and I…we don't talk a lot. Simple as that."

"Aren't you the one," Colin asked, "who told me nothing's simple?"

The man had a tenaciousness that undoubtedly came in handy trying to save somebody's life. But *she* didn't need rescuing, and she didn't want to keep reminding him of it.

"Not that there's anything wrong between my mother and me," she said. "It's just that she's not the most open person in the world. And she's never relished displays of affection. She almost prefers most of our contact to come through Christmas and birthday cards. I gave up fighting her reticence a long time ago."

"Reticence," Colin murmured. "Interesting choice of words."

Alex stood. "You're worse than a first-year psychology student—reading meaning into the most mundane comments.''

"Guess you don't want to talk about it anymore.''

"No,'' she said, her voice taut. "I don't.''

He stood beside her. "Fair enough. It's my turn, Alex. I want to ask you a favor.''

"Really,'' she said noncommittally.

"I want you to come to a baseball game tonight. You, me and Sean.'' He frowned as he spoke.

Alex started walking again, obliging him to follow her. "Colin, just the other day you told me I couldn't make up my mind about you. Well, you're doing almost the same thing. You can't make up your mind about *me*. I'd say that invitation lacked enthusiasm.''

He took her hand and brought her to a halt. "I like being with you, Alex,'' he said quietly. "I like it a lot. And when the time's right, I'm probably going to take you in my arms again.''

Her skin heated as she gazed at him. "Do I have any choice in the matter?''

"Like I said…when the time's right. But if I sounded less than enthusiastic about inviting you, I have a good reason.''

Alex kept gazing at him. She was still back at the part about him taking her in his arms, and she was picturing the scene all too vividly.

He went on. "At first I asked Sean to come to the ball game just with me. He said no. He's been saying that a lot lately. But when I mentioned I might be able to persuade you to come along, he changed his mind. Seems I'm using you to try getting through to my son…and I can't say I like it."

Alex finally had her wayward thoughts under control. "I didn't get the impression last night that Sean was particularly thrilled with me."

"He said yes to a ball game. That's more progress than I've had on my own."

Suddenly a ball game sounded like exactly what she needed. The home team up to bat, the organ playing, vendors hawking peanuts, popcorn and ice-cream sandwiches in the stands.

"I'll go," she said.

With any luck, she'd forget that nightmare.

She might even put it behind her.

CHAPTER FIVE

THE SILVER LAKE MINERS were having a less-than-stellar season. Last week they'd lost their two away games; now they were back in Idaho, trying to recoup. So far they weren't doing a good job: the scoreboard above the left-field fence read Visitors 4, Home 0, and it was the bottom of the fifth.

Colin had forked over an extra fifty cents a ticket so he, Alex and Sean could sit in the stands right above first base. Here the seats had backs and an awning stretched overhead.

He glanced at Alex. She seemed to be enjoying herself, even though she hadn't quite lost the strained look. She was nibbling on a large bag of caramel popcorn. Sean sat next to her, slouching as usual, his feet propped on the seat in front of him. He wore a sullen expression, and had scarcely spoken to either Colin or Alex. Why had he come if he was just going to hunker there like an ill-natured lump? What the hell was wrong with the kid?

Colin realized he had no answers to questions

he'd been asking a lot lately. He tried to concentrate on the game, instead. The Miners' star batter was up—and out. Things definitely weren't looking good.

Three preteen girls tiptoed up the aisle. They stopped in front of Sean, staring at him. Two of them began to giggle. The other one, bolder, held out her program. "Could you...would you..." she stammered.

Sean glanced around as if hoping to see a hole he could disappear into. Finally, when it became clear there was no escape, he took the program and scribbled his signature across the first page.

The girl snatched back the program and darted away. Her two friends scurried after her, shrieking nervously. Sean stuck on his sunglasses and slouched even lower in his seat. Nearby spectators turned to examine Sean, obviously curious about the celebrity who had caused the commotion. Maybe you couldn't blame them—the action out on the field was less than riveting. But Colin couldn't help feeling for his son.

"Sean," Alex said, "would you mind going down to the concession stand for me? I'm still hankering for an ice-cream sandwich, and nobody's selling them up here."

Relief flitted across Sean's face. "Sure," he

mumbled, and disappeared down the aisle in a flash.

"I don't know if getting him out of here will help any," Alex told Colin. "Maybe he'll be mobbed at the concession stand by more girls."

"It was worth a try," Colin said gruffly. "The kid needed a break."

They sat in silence a while longer. The opposing team scored another run.

"You're really worried about him, aren't you?" Alex murmured.

"Yeah, I guess I am. Apparently he was getting into some serious trouble in L.A. The wrong friends, thinking he could do whatever he wanted…telling Beth he made more money than her, so she didn't have any rights over him."

"Ouch."

"Not that long ago all he had was a paper route," Colin said. "Now he makes more money than Beth and me put together."

"Having him come out here to Idaho was probably a smart idea," Alex said thoughtfully.

Colin wished he were as convinced. "Something's got to change. It's not just that he's out of line. It's that he seems unhappy and won't tell anybody why."

By the time the seventh-inning stretch had ar-

rived Sean still hadn't come back from the concession stand.

"He's probably waiting in line," Alex said.
"Give him a little more time, Colin. I don't think
checking up on him would be a good idea."

She was probably right, Colin told himself. He
had to cut Sean a little slack. And so he waited.

"Still think he's standing in line?" Colin asked
at the top of the eighth.

"Okay, he's been gone a long time. But it
doesn't necessarily mean anything."

Colin knew he was probably making a big pro-
duction out of this, the way he usually did when it
came to his son. But he didn't have a good feeling
about Sean right now.

"Be back soon," he said tersely.

Fifteen minutes later, he'd thoroughly searched
the concession stands, the rest rooms and the sta-
dium concourse. No Sean.

He returned to Alex. "Seen him?"

"Not a sign. I'm sorry, Colin. It was my idea to
send him for that ice-cream sandwich—"

"It's not your fault," he told her. Just then the
Miners finally scored a run. Colin, though, was no
longer in any mood to enjoy the game.

His son had ditched him all over again.

MAYBE THERE WAS AN ART to waiting up for a kid
who hadn't come home yet. Maybe you were sup-

posed to distract yourself with a newspaper or a book; maybe you were supposed to do something useful while the hours dragged by. But Colin just sat in the living room of his grandfather's house, not doing anything at all.

A little after midnight, the front door opened. Sean walked past the living room without glancing left or right.

"Hello," Colin said conversationally. Sean paused in the hallway, just beyond Colin's line of sight.

"Talked to your mother earlier." Colin went on, still in that offhand tone. "I called her to ask for a little advice. She told me she didn't have much to offer, unfortunately. She said that when you come home after being out late, she usually loses her cool and hollers at you. That never works too well, though. She says hi, by the way." Colin didn't hear any footsteps going toward Sean's room. Apparently the boy was still listening.

Colin eased back in his armchair, bringing up the footrest. "I've been sitting here, trying to puzzle things out. I figure I have at least a few options. I could yell at you. Not the best option. Or I could just ask what's going on with you—what you're feeling. That option isn't much better. I've tried it before and it hasn't worked." Colin stopped again.

Silence out in the hallway. It was like that time a couple of years back when Colin and his partner had been trying to talk a jumper off a highway overpass. They'd just kept talking and talking, knowing that any false words could be disastrous. Maybe this wasn't a life-and-death situation, but Colin felt the same tense readiness in his nerves...the same need not to say the wrong thing.

"There's a third option," he remarked, "one I *haven't* tried yet. Maybe I'll just sit here and tell you what I think you're feeling. Here goes. The way you bolted from that baseball game tonight— I think you did it for a couple of reasons. One, you wanted to prove to me that you're independent, that you don't have to answer to anybody. Two, after those girls came up to you and asked for your autograph, you just had to get out of there. Basically this celebrity stuff has you really freaked. You hate having strangers recognize you, hate having them stare at you. You can't tell anybody that, because it would mean admitting a weakness. If you could, you'd go back to being ordinary."

Colin had run out of words. And, for the moment, it seemed he'd run out of options. He waited some more. Still, no sound at all from the hallway. Maybe he could chance a move now. He eased the footrest down, stood and went to where he could see his son.

Sean had his head bent, his hands jammed into the pockets of his jeans. But then he jerked his head up and stared at Colin as if he'd been tricked.

"You're wrong," he muttered.

"So why did you leave the game?"

"I felt like it," Sean said.

"Why'd you feel like it?"

Sean hesitated, misery and defiance mingling in his expression. But then, as usual, defiance won out.

"I just felt like it, all right?" He shuffled off toward his room.

For a few seconds, Colin gazed after his son. What would it take to get through to the boy? What burden was he so determined to carry alone?

Sean was just about to disappear into his room.

"Not so fast," Colin said. "We're not finished."

Sean turned and shot him an insolent glance. "I'm finished."

"No. You're grounded."

"Like hell," Sean said.

"From now on, you don't go anywhere unless I'm along."

"You can't tell me what to do."

"In case you forgot," Colin said, "I'm your father."

Sean stared at him some more.

"You're grounded," Colin repeated. "You don't have any choice."

"Yeah, right."

Sean went into his room and shut the door. He seemed to take special care not to bang it, not to give any sign Colin had gotten to him. Maybe he'd already learned that whoever lost his cool was the one most likely to lose the confrontation.

If that was true, then Colin had already lost. Because he was ticked at his son, and more than a little frustrated. And he still didn't know where to go from here.

ALEX LIFTED THE PHONE and dialed the number. And then, after only one ring, hung up.

She felt stupid, the way she had as a child when a friend of hers had convinced her to dial a number at random, say something silly and then slam the receiver down. Only, back then she hadn't been dialing her own mother's house.

The last few minutes, she'd tried rehearsing what she would say. *Hello, Mom. I know I hardly ever call. By the way, could you tell me why suddenly I'm so damn scared of fire?*

Alex walked around her room at the bed-and-breakfast. Then she sat down again and reached for the phone. This time she didn't hang up after she dialed.

"Hello." Gayle Robbins sounded just like she always did when she answered the phone: cautious, a little suspicious of whoever might be on the other end of the line.

"Hi, Mom."

"Alex."

Gayle didn't sound relieved it was only her daughter. Almost involuntarily Alex tightened her hand on the receiver. Why couldn't her mother once—just once—seem delighted to hear her voice?

"How's it going, Mom?"

"Fine. Just fine. I didn't expect to hear from you."

An understatement. Maybe even the birthday card Alex had sent last month had been too big an imposition.

A silence stretched over the wires, and Alex wondered which of them would break it first. Gayle finally gave in.

"How are you, Alex? I was so sorry to hear about you and Jonathan."

"I'm handling it."

More silence. Alex's conversations with Jonathan had often been labored and unsatisfactory like this. It had been a long while since Alex had first seen the similarities between Jonathan and Gayle. Both of them made you work so damn hard for any shred of closeness. Alex had to wonder what that said about *her*. After growing up with a mother like hers, couldn't she have found someone open, someone easy to be with?

She tried again. "How's your job?"

"Just fine. You know Mr. Bryce—always a workaholic. Thinks I should be, too." Gayle worked as an office manager for a law firm, a job she had held for over two decades now.

"Any new projects?" Through trial and error, Alex had learned that this was the least offensive way to refer to her mother's pastimes. Gayle had always had a flair for the artistic, and through the years she'd experimented with beadwork, costume design, woodcutting, printmaking. Her stuff was charming, if offbeat, and seemed to express the emotions that she otherwise kept so restrained.

"I'm doing a little metalwork these days. But don't make it sound important, Alex. You know I just dabble."

Another sore spot between them. Alex always encouraged her mother to take her artwork more seriously and do it full-time, but Gayle always balked. She said she liked the security of the law office; everything else was only a hobby.

When more silence followed, Alex's heart had begun to pound uncomfortably. Now was the time to ask her mother. She *needed* to ask her mother.

Last night she'd had the nightmare again, every detail the same. The fear, the helplessness, the choking in her lungs had been so real she'd jerked awake. And this time there had been actual tears on her cheeks.

She needed her mother's reassurance, needed Gayle to tell her that of course there had never been any fire…that it *was* only a nightmare…

"Mom—"

"Yes, Alex?"

"Just…I just wanted to call and say hello. That's all."

A few seconds later Alex hung up the phone. She pressed her hands to her face and listened to the pounding of her heart.

Part of her wanted to know the truth.

Another part was terrified.

Coward, she told herself.

"THIS IS REALLY COOL," Sean said.

Colin wondered if he'd heard correctly. Was his son really expressing enthusiasm for something?

They were down in the mine with Herb. At the old man's insistence, they were wearing hard hats and carrying a flashlight apiece. Sean panned his light over the damp, dark walls. He almost seemed to be enjoying himself.

Herb led the way down one of the tunnels.

"This is what I'm thinking. All along here, it's already pretty safe. Maybe a few more supports needed, but nothing major. Put them in and I can open for business."

"Herb," Colin said, "I still can't figure out what you're trying to accomplish—"

"I want to make this into a damn tourist attraction, all right? They're doing it with old mines all over the place. People like to slap on a hard hat, go underground for a few minutes and pretend they're being brave. Besides, I can't just let all this go to waste."

He sounded defensive, as if Colin had accused him somehow.

"Cool idea, Grandpa Herbie," said Sean.

The boy seemed to be making an effort to ally himself with his great-grandfather instead of his father. Terrific. A new wrinkle in the McIntyre scheme of things.

"You like it down here, don't you, son?" Herb said approvingly to Sean. "Maybe you can help me get the place ready."

"Thought you were already busy, Herb," Colin interrupted. "What with the hauntings. Not to mention being mayor."

"Coming up with ideas to stimulate tourism *is* part of being mayor." Herb stopped and played his light along the top of the tunnel. "See there, Sean?

That's a good vein of quartz. Did you know gold always runs with quartz? Hoped we'd find some gold down here at one time...but it was always silver that kept us going. We stayed at the mining, too, long past when the other mines were closing. Until we had to close ourselves...I'll never forget the day we had to shut this place down."

More of Herb's timeworn phrases. He'd still been a relatively young man when the McIntyre operation had closed—not yet fifty. He'd had to pursue another line of work—he hadn't had any choice. For years he'd run a small hardware shop in town, and then he'd begun his career in politics. Nothing, however, had ever satisfied him like mining.

"If Thomas had lived," he murmured now, "if only he'd lived...he might have been able to keep this place going for me."

Colin shrugged impatiently, his flashlight arcing across the tunnel walls. "Thomas wasn't a miracle worker. Maybe he was even human."

"I never painted him as a saint," said Herb. "He pushed the limit plenty of times. He knew how to act up."

With Thomas, even acting up had been a virtue—in Herb's eyes, at least.

"There was the time," Herb said, "when

Thomas and his buddies took over that bar in Lewiston…''

Colin had heard the story often before. It seemed Thomas had done no wrong—even when getting plastered.

''He got a little carried away that night,'' Herb was rambling on. ''But it taught him something. In the morning, he told me he never wanted to feel that sick again. And not so long after, he was in Vietnam, proving exactly what he was made of.''

Colin felt the familiar frustration. Whenever he tried to get beneath his father's image, he bumped up against Herb's stories.

''Hell, I know your dad wasn't perfect,'' Herb said. ''But if he fell down, he got up again. Why do you want something different?''

An impossible question to answer. Thomas had died so long ago. Did it really matter anymore what kind of person he'd been? Colin would always regret that he hadn't had a father most of the time he was growing up. But it was an old regret. Wasn't it time to let it go?

''Never mind,'' Colin said.

''People aren't replaceable, you know,'' Herb said in a low voice. ''You can't lose somebody and then just…forget.''

What could Colin say to that? Herb was probably the most loyal person he'd ever known. A loyalty that enduring, that persistent…you could only call it admirable.

"Where'd the boy go to?" Herb asked.

Sean was nowhere to be seen. Colin swore under his breath. He'd gotten so involved talking about Thomas he hadn't even noticed his son had disappeared.

"Sean," he called, his voice echoing. "Sean, get back here."

"No need for excitement," Herb said. "My guess is that he snuck outside, just to give us a hard time. I'll go check." Herb went back along the tunnel. But he returned in only a few moments.

"No sign of him out there."

Colin swore again. "We know he didn't go farther down this tunnel—we were blocking the way. Exactly how many other tunnels are there?"

"Enough," Herb said tersely.

"Dammit, I told him to stick close."

"I told him, too, didn't I? We just have to start looking. No need to get excited," Herb repeated.

But he sounded worried. He didn't say what Colin already knew: a whole lot of this mine was no longer safe.

"How easy would it be for Sean to get lost down here?"

"If he's smart," Herb said, "he'll turn around and find us again…before he gets too deep."

"You know Sean. What are the odds of that?"

"Damn stubborn boy of yours," Herb muttered. "Always trying to prove some point about his independence."

"Okay," Colin said grimly. "We have to be systematic about searching for him. You know this mine. Where do we start?"

"Back along here." Herb was surefooted and moved remarkably quickly. "This is the first turn he'd be likely to take…"

There was a problem with tunnels. To the uninitiated, they all looked alike. Not to mention the fact that you lost your sense of direction underground. Colin knew it all too well. That long-ago day when he was eight years old and he'd snuck off to explore the mine on his own, he'd started out cocky. It hadn't taken long to go from cocky to scared, though.

Now Colin followed Herb, having to depend on his grandfather's knowledge. But he didn't like not being the one in control. When he worked, he wanted to be in charge, leading the rescue effort.

Except this wasn't a rescue, Colin told himself. It was just his son being difficult again, trying to prove he didn't need anybody else—not even his own family. Just a few minutes and he would appear.

The few minutes turned into half an hour. Colin

and Herb called Sean's name as they went down first one tunnel, then another. Herb chose his way unerringly, but no answer came from Sean, no flashlight glimmered just ahead. There was only the darkness of the mine. It was as if the mine had swallowed up Sean.

Colin thought back to when his son was little—maybe three, four years old. Then, he'd known you couldn't take your eyes off the kid for a second. That was all Sean needed to vanish. So, Colin and Beth had watched him and it became second nature for them to have the boy always in their sight. Maybe that drove you crazy as a parent, but you did it. You did whatever you had to do to keep your child from harm. And you looked forward to the years when maybe, just maybe, you could relax your vigilance a little.

But maybe you couldn't relax it—even with a boy of fifteen. Colin swore yet again.

"I know," Herb said. "I'm going to throttle the kid, too, when we find him."

If they ever did...

CHAPTER SIX

THE SILVER LAKE COMMUNITY Library was something of a misnomer. The place was one small room, tucked behind the county clerk's office… and it didn't even have any windows. The Psychology section consisted of precisely three dusty volumes.

Alex sat at the only table, slowly turning the pages of a 1948 text on the psyche of the chimp. So much for researching repressed memory and finding something to help her figure out if she was hiding secrets deep in her subconscious.

Alex felt ridiculous sitting there at all. It occurred to her that she far preferred delving into other people's emotional problems than her own. A psychologist trying to diagnose herself! She might as well be an orthopedic surgeon trying to set her own broken leg.

So maybe she should consult a therapist. Not an easy thing to do, however. Silver Lake had a few social workers, but not one bona fide psychologist.

Alex knew, because she'd already checked the phone listings.

I don't want to talk to anyone about it anyway. I just want it to go away.

The thought came unbidden to her. One part of her still insisted that she learn the truth. Another part of her, equally insistent, told her to leave well enough alone.

She closed the musty book, then pushed her chair back and left the library. Her legs felt cramped from sitting too long, so she walked briskly down the street, toward the shore. For a moment she was reminded of Chicago, curving its way around Lake Michigan. Here was another town—much smaller, admittedly—tucked right against a shoreline. Alex was drawn to water. She couldn't imagine not living near an ocean or a lake.

She laughed a little to herself. Water…the opposite of fire, you could say. Was that why it attracted her?

No more self-analysis. She hadn't had the nightmare last night; she'd slept deeply. She couldn't remember having any dreams at all. So why was she so jumpy today?

She reached the lake, where a park fronted the narrow beach. On impulse, she took off her shoes, rolled up her pant legs and waded into the water. It felt cool and comforting against her skin.

A moment later she continued walking along the shore, now and then allowing the water to lap at her feet. The mountains rose above the lake, cloaked in green. There'd been a time when she couldn't imagine living without mountains. In Montana, the mountains had been a part of her life...always there, rising against the horizon.

But she'd left Montana just as soon as she was old enough. She hardly ever went back. She hated going back.

Alex stopped where she was, the water eddying at her ankles. Her heart had started to pound in that all-too-familiar way, and she could hardly catch her breath. She was inexplicably frightened again, this time in the middle of a beautiful summer day.

She knew something, though. She didn't know *how* she knew it, but the knowledge was suddenly there.

Whatever frightened her was in Montana.

''WHAT THE HELL DID YOU think you were doing?''

Colin had told himself that he wasn't going to get angry. His first reaction to finding Sean in one of those tunnels was sheer, intense relief. His second reaction was to get his kid aboveground.

His third reaction was anger.

Sean sat down in the dirt, knees jutting awkwardly. He looked a little white himself.

"I didn't mean to go very far away. It just... happened."

"Cut the bull. It's the same damn thing you did last night at the game."

Sean glared at him. "It wasn't, all right? I just wanted to look around a little. And you and Herbie were talking about the same old crap—"

"Watch your mouth," said Herb. He looked shaken, too, as if suddenly he felt all of his seventy-six years. "I don't care what your excuse is. I told you—that mine is dangerous. You were supposed to stay with us."

"Yeah, well...you were talking about the same old cr...crud."

"All kinds of things can happen down there," Herb said roughly. "A piece of timber that doesn't hold, a little bad air, a too-close encounter with one of the vertical shafts...anything." He sat down on a tree stump and took off his miner's hat, then pushed a hand through his rumpled white hair. "Look, when your dad was a kid and *he* got lost in the mine...lucky thing we found him. And you're one lucky kid, too."

Sean didn't answer. He just clamped his hands on his knees, as the color slowly returned to his face.

Colin didn't even want to consider the possibility of his son being gone. His anger faded. "You're grounded double," he said.

"Yeah, right."

"Kid's got a point," said Herbie. "What're you going to do, put a leash on him?"

Colin hadn't expected dissension from his grandfather—not after what the two of them had just been through.

"I'll do whatever it takes. But from now on, he doesn't leave my sight."

"You're just setting up a challenge to him. He'll get away from you sooner or later. You have to sleep sometime, don't you?"

Colin stared at his grandfather. "Herb, what's this all about?"

"I've been thinking the two of you aren't getting much of anywhere. Don't get me wrong, Colin—I see all the efforts you make with the kid. You try one tactic, then you try another. You're always looking for an angle. You haven't found one yet—but hey, you're trying. And you, Sean— you don't even give your dad a chance."

Colin reminded himself that next time he wanted to exert some parental authority, he should do it without his grandfather around.

"Herb, you probably mean well, but this is between Sean and me—"

"I'm not part of the family?" Herb said grouchily. "Last time I checked, I was head of the family. Don't you remember when *you* acted up as a kid and I straightened you out?"

That took Colin back. It had been after his father's death. His grief had come out as rebelliousness, until his mother hadn't known what to do with him. But Herb, in his gruff way, had understood. Despite his own grief, he'd provided the male influence Colin had needed.

"I remember," Colin said.

"I've been thinking," Herb mused. "Why not let Sean spend a little more time with me? He'll still be grounded...but he can help me out some in the mine—"

"As far as I'm concerned, he's never going down in that damn place again."

"Now, that's where you're wrong, Colin," said Herb. "Boy needs to learn the proper respect for the mine. I'll show him how. Besides, you know that as long as he sticks with me, he'll be safe."

"I'll do it," Sean said.

Colin glanced at his son. "I'm supposed to believe you'll follow orders—"

"Yeah. Grandpa Herbie can count on me."

"There—you heard him. He'll do what I say. *You* did, didn't you?"

Colin couldn't deny what he knew from personal

experience. Herb had a way of making youngsters pay attention. But Colin still didn't like putting his grandfather that much in charge of his son.

"Got any better ideas?" Herb asked.

That was the clincher. Colin studied Herb again, still not quite sure what the old man was up to. Then he saw the way his grandfather looked at Sean, his expression just a little wistful, and he started to understand. If you put a photograph of Sean right beside a photo of Thomas at that same age, you'd see a striking similarity.

Now Colin studied Sean. Herb was right about one thing: Colin had been trying all kinds of ways to get through to his son, and so far nothing had worked.

"You'll do whatever Herb tells you?"

"Sure. Why not?"

Maybe it would give Colin and Sean some breathing space, a chance to be father and son without Colin always telling Sean to shape up and Sean always running away. At this point, Colin was willing to do anything.

"We'll try it," he said. "That's all—we'll give it a try."

ALEX FOLLOWED COLIN up the slope of the mountain, then stopped and frowned at him.

"What's the big idea?" she said. "I thought you'd consented to an interview."

Funny how people could have different perceptions. The way Colin saw it, he'd invited Alex on an outing this afternoon. Okay, maybe she'd mentioned wanting to talk, and he'd agreed, but he hadn't seen it as an "interview."

"Don't tell me you packed your tape recorder for a hike up the mountain," he said.

She shifted her unwieldy canvas bag from one shoulder to the other. "I didn't know we were going on a hike. You have this aggravating way of surprising me, Colin."

"It's just a little farther." He went up the winding path, with Alex close behind. And then they came to a clearing.

"At last," he said, gazing at the weathered gray walls of the old wooden church before him, the hand-carved cross presiding above the front gable, the purple and yellow wildflowers tangling at the steps. "At last something around here's stayed the way I remember it."

"Nice."

"A Jesuit priest built this church almost single-handedly back in the 1870s," he told her. "Father Matthew something-or-other. He came out here to convert the miners. I don't know if he succeeded, but apparently he liked the place. Even after the silver collapse, when most of his parishioners left, he stayed on. He's buried in the graveyard around back.'' Colin led Alex around the side of the church, where grass and nettles threatened to overrun the scattered gravestones. He pointed out the simple cross that marked the priest's resting place.

"Thanks for bringing me here," Alex murmured. "It's lovely and peaceful, and I think I needed something like that."

Today she had that strained look again. "Another nightmare?" he asked.

"No. The *same* nightmare. I thought it was giving me some time off. Then last night, all over again."

But she didn't seem to want to talk about it, and now she was the one who led the way. They wandered into the church. A thick layer of dust had settled over the pews, the planked floor, the simple altar. A few yellowed pictures were still tacked to the walls, their edges curling and brittle. Alex appeared deep in thought. When they went back outside, she sank onto the church steps and didn't speak for a long while. Colin settled beside her. The cool, pine-laden air drifted around them. At last, Alex sighed.

"I can see why someone wouldn't want to leave here. At times I wish I could find a place like this…a place I didn't want to leave."

"Chicago's not doing the job?" he asked.

"I love Chicago. It's just that it's never felt like home. Montana never did, either, even though I grew up there. Makes me realize that I'm…rootless." She drew her eyebrows together.

"You could always settle down in Idaho."

"Too close to Montana," she said promptly. Then, making an obvious effort to change the subject, she reached into her canvas bag and brought out a notepad. "You did say we could talk, Colin."

"Thought we already were."

She looked at him consideringly. "You're always telling me how observant you are. Well, I'm observant, too. And I can tell something's bugging you."

"Chalk it up to my grandfather and my son. They've decided to be buddies. Even as we speak, Herb is teaching Sean the ins and outs of being a silver miner."

"That sounds like something good." Alex reached into her bag again and rummaged around until she found a pen.

"It should be good, but it doesn't feel that way. I grounded Sean big time, and yesterday Herb finagled his way into being the kid's prison guard. He seems to like the job—I think Sean reminds him of my dad. You're not going to write this down, are you?''

"Hmm, family problems of the Type R male. I'm not working on that chapter yet," she said solemnly, "but the subject's intriguing."

"Not all that intriguing," he muttered. "I'd just like to know why my grandfather and my son are suddenly getting along…and I can't get along with either of them."

She tapped her pen against the pad. "Let's back up a little. You mentioned something interesting. You said Sean reminds Herb of your father. But—''

"Is this part of the interview?"

"Don't break my train of thought," she said sternly. "Here's the thing. All you McIntyres have a marked likeness. So you must remind Herbie of your father, too. Only, you didn't mention that. I wonder why."

The topic wasn't exactly a comfortable one. "What do you say we drop it, Alex."

Now she had a stubborn look. "Avoiding problems won't get you anywhere, Colin."

"Is that what you tell all your patients?"

"Hey, I'm not psychoanalyzing you," she said almost defensively. "But when I see a problem, I want to kick it around."

"There's no problem," he told her. "I always

knew my grandfather cared for me in his own way, but he never considered me as any substitute for Thomas. Still, it's been a long time since Thomas died. And maybe at last Herb can see that his son left some kind of legacy. Namely, Sean.''

"Why not you?'' she persisted. "You're a legacy, too, aren't you?''

He smiled just a little. "Can't say I ever thought of myself that way. But Herb probably thinks it's too late for me to live up to my father's image.''

"Is that why you went into rescue work?'' Alex murmured. "To live up to the image?''

Colin couldn't say he liked this interview business. "Hell, that's not news to me. It's why I joined the air force first chance I could—thought I was going to be exactly like my dad. Sure, I got out as soon as I realized I didn't like some guy in an officer's uniform telling me what to do. But even after that, I kept trying to follow in the footsteps of Thomas McIntyre. Think I need a shrink to tell me as much?''

Alex didn't write anything down. She merely went on thoughtfully tapping her pen against the notepad. Colin stood, the old restlessness dogging him. He pulled Alex up beside him, and her pen fell to the ground. Just as well, he figured.

"I didn't come here to talk about Thomas. I get enough of that from Herb.''

"So why *are* we here?"

"Because we both wanted to get away," he said. "We both needed a break." He brought her into his arms, but she placed her hands against his chest, resisting.

"Colin, you said you weren't going to do this until…until the time was right…"

"The time is right."

She gazed at him another moment, her brown eyes very dark. And then she brought her arms around his neck and lifted her face to his.

ALEX INDULGED. She stood on the steps of the church and she kissed Colin. She twined her fingers in his hair and trembled when his fingers brushed her cheek. Warmth flooded her veins, weakened her knees. And still she indulged.

At last she recollected herself and pulled away. "Not in front of a *church*, Colin. Among other things, I'm still married. Technically, at least." Then she hurried down the steps.

He followed her into the clearing and took her hand. "If it's just a technicality…"

"Look, Colin, as soon as I get those papers and I read the words that say I'm no longer his wife…I'm going to celebrate being a divorcée. I'll have earned it, believe me."

He nodded thoughtfully. "I get it. You want to

enjoy your freedom. You don't want to tie yourself down with the likes of me.''

She wished Colin's touch wouldn't have such an effect on her. He just had to hold her hand and she went weak at the knees.

''If *you'd* been living with someone who made you feel you were under a dark cloud all the time...wouldn't you want a little freedom, too?''

''You said the guy used to get angry,'' Colin reminded her. ''Are you afraid he'd be angry now, if he saw you with me?''

''That doesn't have anything to do with it.'' But she knew she'd answered too quickly. Merely thinking about Jonathan's moods made her stomach tighten. He'd always had a good reason for his ill temper—career disappointments, troubles with his family. But whereas other people eventually rebounded, Jonathan had grown more and more irritable. And, more and more, he had refused all of Alex's efforts to help.

''After Jonathan...I just have to be on my own for a while. Can you understand?''

''I know one thing,'' Colin said. ''You're better off without him.''

She rubbed her arms, the afternoon suddenly cool. ''Somehow I'm not bubbling over with joy,'' she said caustically. ''How can I be, with that wretched nightmare...and with *you*...''

"You're saying I haven't brought a whole lot of cheer into your life?"

The locale didn't seem so peaceful anymore. The mountainside church felt lonely, abandoned. "I thought I was doing all right," she said quietly. "But then I saw that video…and I met you. I'm not sure of anything anymore. The way you make me feel…"

He stepped close to her. "How do I make you feel, Alex?"

This time she couldn't even look into his eyes. "Raw," she answered in a low voice. "Uncertain. Scared. And…wanting." She wished she hadn't let that last bit slip out. Because already Colin was taking her into his arms once more.

"I'm wanting, too," he said.

Then he kissed her, as if that could solve all their problems. And she kissed him back, even though she knew it wouldn't solve anything at all.

ALEX'S FINGERS CLICKED over the keyboard of her laptop computer. Then she paused to read what she'd written so far. Exasperated, she shook her head and hit the Delete key yet again.

Why did she stumble with words whenever she tried to describe Colin? He was, after all, the Type R male personified: strong-willed, supremely con-

fident, undeniably dogmatic, recklessly handsome...

The Type R male, she reminded herself, did not
need to be handsome. That was just a bonus in
Colin's case. Yet she still couldn't turn him into a
research subject. He refused to settle down on the
page.

Hoping for inspiration, she opened a folder con-
taining paperwork on her research grant. A private
foundation in Chicago had awarded her a respect-
able sum to study the Type R male. But the foundation required regular progress reports. It did not
expect her to fritter away her time in Idaho.

After a few moments she opened another file
and extracted some newspaper clippings. She
spread them around her, then referred to them as
she typed. They were all about how Colin had rescued those people in the Bayview blaze. He and
his partner had arrived at the burning apartment
complex ahead of the local fire department. Colin
hadn't waited for the proper equipment. He'd been
the first on the fire escape, only to have one of the
ladders jam so he couldn't pull it down. That
hadn't stopped him. He'd broken a window and
crawled inside. His partner had followed. Together,
the two of them made their way up stairwells
clogged with deadly smoke. They'd rescued that
young child, an elderly couple, two young teenag-

ers, a woman—and a cat. By the time the whole thing was over, Colin and his partner had almost lost their lives. The smoke hadn't killed them, but the fire itself nearly had. Colin's partner had suffered second-degree burns.

Alex stared at the computer screen. Now the blaze sprang to life for her all too vividly. Her heartbeat accelerated, and she asked the question that tormented her more and more: *What's wrong with me?*

She saved the document and turned off the computer. Only then did her heartbeat return to normal. She felt foolish. Glancing at her watch, she was surprised to see that it was almost seven-thirty. Colin had brought her back from their outing over three hours ago, and she'd been trying to work ever since—for all the good it had done her. She'd managed to write only that one paragraph, yet all the while Colin had filled her thoughts.

Careful, a voice inside her warned. *Watch out, or you'll fall for another difficult man. Then where will you be?*

Alex propped her head in her hands. First, she told herself, she wasn't falling for Colin. Second, he wasn't anything like Jonathan—he didn't guard his emotions like tarnished treasure.

But he was still a difficult man.

He risked his neck for a living, he left beautiful

women in his wake and he made Alex feel as if she were tumbling free fall off a mountaintop.

Plus, she'd only had that nightmare since meeting *him*.

The phone rang, startling her. She pushed back her chair and went to answer it. She was somewhat surprised when she heard who was on the other end of the line. Surprised, but pleased, too.

"Yes, I do know how...well, yes, I suppose I could...right now, you mean? Why, yes...I'd like that. I'll be right over."

CHAPTER SEVEN

ALEX WAS MORE THAN a decent poker player. Aggressive, too. You could never tell when she was bluffing or when she had a killer hand.

Herb shook his head as Alex raked in the chips.

"I should have realized this was a mistake," he said. "Never...never play poker with a woman who shows up with her own deck of cards. Maybe it *was* a mistake to ask you over, Dr. Alex."

"I always carry a deck when I'm traveling," she said. "For solitaire, you know." She dealt the next hand, deuces wild.

Colin glanced around the table. Herb had the absorbed look he always wore when he played cards. Sean had the same lousy posture as always—hunched over. But he actually seemed relaxed. And Alex sat among the McIntyre males as if perfectly comfortable. She'd pulled her hair into a ponytail, but one rebellious strand dangled at her cheek. If they'd been alone, Colin would have smoothed the hair back from her face and they would have proceeded from there. Unfortunately they weren't.

Colin asked for three cards, knew he couldn't have a worse hand if he tried and folded. He went out to the kitchen for more chips and soda. A few minutes later, Herb poked his head through the doorway.

"I'm out, too. It's just Sean and your girlfriend now."

"She's not my girlfriend," Colin remarked as he tore open a package of potato chips.

"Could've fooled me. You must like keeping her to yourself—you sure resent me inviting her tonight."

The old man didn't miss much, it seemed.

"She doesn't belong to me, Herb. You can invite her all you like."

Herb went to the fridge and peered in. "Too bad you're not being honest with yourself. You like her better than any lady you've met since Beth."

Colin dumped the chips into a bowl. "Don't tell me this whole thing is a matchmaking effort."

"Hell, no. I invited her because she's good company. Your kid thinks she's good company, too, though he'd probably never admit it." Herb took some French onion dip out of the fridge and popped off the lid.

"Sean been giving you any trouble?"

"I already told you—he's fine. The two of us have an understanding. He does what I tell him."

Somehow that didn't sound promising to Colin. Yet he couldn't deny that the McIntyre household was a little more peaceful. Sean seemed to be toeing the line. Problem was, Colin didn't like abdicating any part of parenthood...even when parenthood drove him crazy.

Herb went back into the living room with the French onion dip. Colin followed with the chips and a six-pack of cherry soda. The pile of poker chips in front of Sean had grown bigger. His expression was carefully indifferent, even though Colin knew the boy was like everybody else in the family—he loved to win.

Herb shuffled the cards. They played a few more hands, ate all the chips. Herb and Sean got into a bidding war; Alex and Colin folded.

"Mind if I get something else to eat?" she asked him. "I only had a quick sandwich for dinner, and this game is working up my appetite."

"We'll find you something." He and Alex went back to the kitchen, and this time she was the one to peer in the fridge.

"Do you guys eat *anything* besides steak?"

"Could've sworn I saw some egg salad in there somewhere. Herb makes a good egg salad."

Alex found it, along with a loaf of light rye. "Care to join me?"

"No, thanks." He got a plate for her, and she placed two pieces of bread on it. She looked at him thoughtfully.

"You don't like me making myself at home, do you?"

Apparently he was sending out all the wrong signals tonight. "I like it fine, Alex."

"No, you don't." She spread egg salad on one piece of bread, then the other. "This is family territory, and you figure I'm intruding."

"Maybe it's the other way around. Maybe I feel the family's intruding." What Herb had said was true—he liked having Alex to himself. He wanted what he had with her to be something apart from the rest of his life. After all, the rest of his life wasn't something to shout about at the moment.

Alex piled her sandwich halves together, then opened a few drawers until she found a knife. "I'm doing it again—acting like this place is my own. But your grandfather makes me feel at home." She cut her sandwich in two. "I don't understand why, exactly. He's brusque, but I feel I've known him a long while."

"He can have that effect on people."

She rinsed the knife and put it in the dish drainer. "Bottom line—I still get the feeling you

don't want me here with your family, Colin.
Maybe I suspected all along that you wouldn't like
it, but...I guess I didn't want to be alone tonight.''

''You should've told me that. We could have
done something about it.''

She gave him a sharp glance. ''Being alone with
you isn't the answer. Not for either one of us.''

''Maybe it is the answer.''

She gazed at him. He could tell by the way her
eyes darkened that she knew what he was thinking.

''No, Colin,'' she said at last. ''*That* isn't the
answer.'' Her voice wavered just a little. Then she
grabbed her sandwich and left.

ALEX DIALED HER MOTHER'S telephone number,
then listened to the rings. One, two...five, six.
Eight... She felt a mixture of disappointment and
relief. Making this call had taken a lot of willpower. On the other hand, if her mother didn't answer Alex would be able to delay the confrontation
just a little while longer.

''Hello?'' Gayle Robbins picked up on the four-
teenth ring, sounding breathless and perhaps resentful.

''Hello, Mom.''

''Alex?''

''Did I disturb you?''

"No, of course not," Gayle said, making it clear that Alex *had* disturbed her.

"Look, Mom, I'll get right to the point. I have a question to ask you." Alex took a deep breath, filled with a nameless dread. "Could you tell me...this is going to sound absurd. But—have I ever been in a fire?" There. Somehow she'd gotten it out. Yet the dread didn't go away.

A long, long silence stretched at the other end of the line.

"Mom, are you still there?"

"Of course I am." Gayle was irritated. "I'm just wondering why you'd ask that out of the blue. It seems so unusual."

Alex gripped the receiver. "Yes, I suppose it does. But you see, lately I've been having this nightmare. It's always the same. I'm curled up in bed, and there's a fire, and I can't move... Look, I know how ridiculous it sounds, but I have to know if it's a nightmare—or if I'm remembering something. And you're the only one who can tell me."

"For goodness' sake, Alex." Gale sounded exasperated. "Are you accusing me of hiding something from you?"

"I'm not accusing you, Mom. I'm just asking—"

"Don't you think I would tell you anything you needed to know?"

Now Alex was the one who remained silent. Perhaps Gayle was reserved, perhaps she kept most of her thoughts and feelings to herself, but why *would* she hide something important?

"Alex, you may not believe this, but I've always had your best interests at heart. You are my daughter, after all."

"Yes," Alex said wryly, "I am your daughter."

"I would feel very hurt to think you didn't trust me."

That was something else Gayle shared with Jonathan—the ability to lay on the guilt at the most effective moment.

"I trust you," Alex said. "That's never been the problem between us."

"I wasn't aware there *was* a problem." Gayle spoke sharply.

"Maybe there isn't."

"Maybe? Alex, if you have a complaint, I wish you'd just say it straight out."

Alex sighed. How adeptly her mother had turned this conversation away from Alex's questions. She was making it seem as if Alex had called to harass her.

"Mom, I just thought something happened to me when I was a kid. Maybe when I was so young

I couldn't remember it...at least not consciously. And I thought maybe that was where the nightmare was coming from.''

"I've already given you my answer, Alex. I am not a devious person.''

Their goodbyes were strained. Alex hung up, and buried her head in her hands. Maybe she should trust her mother after all, and just get on with her life.

But she had a distressing conviction that was growing stronger by the minute. Her mother *was* hiding something from her. Something important.

HALF AN HOUR LATER, Alex swung on the porch swing at the bed-and-breakfast. She was making a great effort to empty her mind of all disturbing thoughts and she found the movement of the swing soothing. But then Tina Scott came breezing out onto the porch, as stunning as ever. She was carrying a watering can, and she began dousing the potted geraniums, daisies and begonias that lined the porch.

"So...does he talk about me?''

Alex used the tip of her foot to keep rocking. "Does who talk about you?'' she asked pointedly.

"You know who. *Him.*''

"Tina, I've already told you. Colin and I have

a professional relationship. I don't ask him about his romantic life.''

''Well, I'm glad to hear that your relationship is *professional*. Word about town has it otherwise. But you're his shrink, aren't you? So why wouldn't you ask him about his love life?''

Alex stifled a groan. ''Tina...I am not his shrink. And if you want him back, I'm afraid you'll have to do it without any help from me.''

Tina set down her watering can and perched on the railing. She wore a blouse in turquoise silk, black jeans and suede boots—hardly the attire for garden duty. But she looked smashing, and no doubt knew it.

''Alex, let's not beat around the bush. We both know you're my competition when it comes to hunk-of-the-century Colin McIntyre. Hey, it's not like I *mind* a little competition. I just like to be aboveboard about it.''

This time Alex did groan. ''I'll make it easy for you, okay? The playing field's all yours. Have at it.''

Tina shrugged. ''Let's not make it too easy, shall we? Getting guys too easily has been the problem my entire life. Why do you think I appreciate Colin so much? He was always hard to get, even back in the days when we had a thing going.''

Alex hated herself for it, but she couldn't help

being curious. "So you're saying you pursued him instead of the other way around."

Tina leaned back against one of the posts, gazing dreamily at the lawn. "I'm not ashamed to admit it. Every summer he'd come back to town, and every summer I'd have to start in on him all over again. He was quite a challenge. I had to keep pretending that I saw our whole relationship as a lark. Only way not to scare him off, I suppose. But here's the joke, Alex. Every summer, I fell for him—fell really hard. It would take me the rest of the year to get over him...and then he'd show up in town all over again. The last time, I don't think I *did* get over him. Perhaps I've never stopped loving him."

Tina suddenly went quiet. She remained in profile, as if purposefully not looking at Alex, staring sadly off into space. Was she doing it just for effect? Or was she really in love with Colin?

Alex didn't know the answer, but she almost sympathized with the woman. Tina had something engaging about her. Maybe it was her casual acceptance of her own good looks, or her habit of saying exactly what was on her mind.

Now she drew a small cream envelope out of her shirt pocket and handed it to Alex. "You'll give this to him, won't you?"

"Tina—"

"It's a letter."

"I can see that," Alex said.

"A letter from me to Colin. You might as well know I confess everything to him in there. So, if you'd just deliver it…"

"Tina, ever heard of the U.S. Postal Service?"

"It would be so much more effective if *you* gave it to him." Tina hopped off the railing. "Thanks, Alex. You're really a friend, you know that?"

And, before Alex could object, she went sailing back into the house, her watering can abandoned on the front porch railing.

ALEX HAD HAD THE NIGHTMARE again. This time it had washed over her with a sickening sensation. She'd awoken feeling as if she'd dragged herself through clouds of smoke.

Now she slipped on her robe, went to close the window to the coolness of the night air, then sank wearily into a bedside chair. She already knew from experience that she wouldn't be able to sleep again for a long while. Her only remedy for insomnia was to open the latest mystery she'd bought at the drugstore.

Alex had never before understood why people liked mysteries. She understood now, though. Knowing that the crime, no matter how puzzling, would always be solved by the last page of the book was comforting. So different from her own life... What if *her* questions were never answered?

But she wouldn't think about that now. With determination she began reading, turning one page after another. The story drew her in, lulled her. She tried to let the night pass unheeded...those hours so far from dawn you wonder if day will ever come. And at last she did sleep, her head resting against the back of the chair, the book slipping from her fingers. No nightmare this time...

She awoke hours later, her neck stiff from the awkward position. The sky was still dark. Groggily she picked up her book, yawning wearily. But only a few moments later, a tapping sounded at her window.

"What on earth...?" She went to the window and peered out. Colin McIntyre stood there, illuminated by the porch light. She yanked up the window and leaned out. "Colin," she whispered fiercely, "what the heck are you doing here?"

"I was driving around...thinking. Saw your light on."

"How did you know it was my light?"

"Easy," Colin said. "Everyone knows Tina reserves this room for people she wants to impress." He looked dissatisfied. "Tonight I wasn't getting much sleep, either."

"Something bugging you?"

"Maybe," he said. "Maybe not. You're the psychologist. Come help me find out."

Alex cinched her robe tighter. "You're crazy," she said. "It's the middle of the night."

Colin leaned in the window, putting his hands on the sill. "It's the middle of a cool Idaho night...and we're both too restless to sleep. Why not come with me, Alex? What do you have to lose?"

She hesitated, but curiosity got the better of her. "Okay, okay. But give me a minute. I look a mess."

Colin leaned closer still. "Could have fooled me," he said.

Alex drew the curtains abruptly on him and went to splash water over her face. Then she donned jeans, a pullover, a fleece jacket, her sneakers. After giving her hair the required brushing, she slipped outside.

Colin put his arm around her shoulders as they walked toward the Jeep.

"What's this for?" she asked.

"No special reason. Just something that needed doing." He ushered her into his Jeep, and before she knew it they were driving along the dark streets of Sobriety.

"What *is* this all about?" she asked, trying to sound grouchy.

"You'll see," he said.

"Oh, no. Another surprise?"

"Afraid so." He headed out of Sobriety, and soon the miles were flying under the Jeep.

She must have dozed. When she opened her eyes, she realized they were driving through the town of Silver Lake. Colin didn't stop, though. He continued on through the outskirts, then they turned onto a dirt road that bordered the lake.

Before long Colin pulled to a stop in front of a house perched on a slope that led right down to the lake. The sun had risen by now for Alex to make out a red shingle roof, trim white clapboards and a bay window on either side of the main door.

"Here it is," he said. "The big surprise."

"It's a great house. But I still don't understand what we're doing here."

"The place is mine," he said gruffly. "Bid's accepted, check's cashed and closing won't take long. Since the former owner's already vacated...I'm free to take possession anytime."

"Wow," she said. "Guess you've been thinking about this for a while."

"I knew I needed something different in my life. I just didn't expect to buy a house...especially not here in Idaho."

"You act like the place took you unawares, Colin."

He ran a hand through his hair, looking perplexed. "I don't usually buy anything on impulse. What the hell got into me?"

"Let's find out," she said. "Take me on the grand tour."

Together they climbed out of the Jeep, and he led her through the house. She found it as undeniably charming inside as out: pine floors, carved moldings, window seats, a second story with three snug bedrooms, even a finished attic where you could have a hideaway right under the eaves. And always that view of the lake, with the morning sun turning the water a warm copper-rose.

She and Colin returned to the first floor, and she sank onto one of the window seats. Colin stood in front of her.

"It just hit me," he said. "I bought this place because of you."

She stared at him. *"Me—"*

"Sure. You're the one who started talking about what it would be like to have a place where you belonged…a place you wouldn't want to leave. You made it sound like a rite of passage."

"I remember," she said. "We were up at the church, talking about Father Matthew whatever and how *he'd* found a place where he belonged…and how contented he must have been all his life…" A wistfulness came over her, and she tried to fight it. "I still don't see what this house has to do with me."

Colin glanced around reflectively. "You made me think, that's all. You made me wonder if maybe it's time for me to settle down."

Alex studied him. Nothing about his appearance gave the impression of someone who could "settle down." That thick dark hair worn long at the collar, those intense blue eyes, the expression that always hinted of unrest... No, the settled image definitely didn't fit.

"Forget settling down, Colin," she said. "You're not the type."

"'Type' again." He shook his head. "Beats the hell out of me," he muttered. "But I have to face facts. I have a fifteen-year-old son and I've lived in an apartment since the divorce. I keep changing jobs because I get bored by the same old thing. I do love the mountains—and this *is* the prettiest lake in the country. Maybe I just need a place where I belong, a place where I can settle in."

"Settling *in* might suit you more than settling *down*," she acknowledged. "Call it a summer house and I'll think you've made a terrific decision. Call it settling down, and I'll think you're nuts."

"Doing something halfway doesn't make sense, Alex. Either I live here full-time, or I don't."

"Wait a minute," she said. "What about your job in California?"

"I've known for a while it's time to move on."

Alex gazed out at the water again. "But, Colin—if you quit your job, what're you going to do? You can't just sit by the lake all day."

"I haven't thought that far ahead," he grumbled. "I just bought the damn place on impulse."

"This corner of Idaho's on the quiet side," she reminded him.

"So maybe I should be looking for quiet." He seemed disgruntled.

"Colin, you'd better accept it. You're the classic Type R male. And Type R men are *never* satisfied with quiet."

"Not that again."

"On the spur of the moment," she said, "maybe it sounds okay—settling back, settling in, whatever you want to call it. But the challenge just wouldn't be enough for you. Because that's what the Type R male thrives on—challenge."

Colin gave Alex a look that told her he'd heard enough about the Type R male. He took her hand and drew her to him. "I've already admitted slapping a down payment on this place was probably a crazy thing to do. Can't explain it myself— maybe I should have my head examined. Of course, if that's the case—you *are* a psychologist.

You're the lady for the job. Maybe you and I could spend the day here together. Figure things out...''

"The whole day—alone with you..."

"Got any better plans?" he asked.

Unfortunately she didn't. She was entirely free to spend the day with this dangerously handsome Type R man. Worst of all...she wanted to spend the day with him.

CHAPTER EIGHT

A FISHING BOAT HAD COME with the house, but Colin explained that he hadn't had time to buy a fishing rod yet. Now he and Alex just drifted in the middle of the lake, water lapping against the boat. Alex felt as if she could stay out here for hours.

"Still think I'm crazy?" Colin asked.

She trailed her hand in the water. "Again...call this a summer getaway and I'll think you're the smartest person in the world."

"If you're going to change your life, summers alone won't do the job."

Alex winced. "That reminds me." She reached down to the floor of the boat, where she'd left her tote bag. After rummaging through it, she pulled out the small cream envelope with Colin's name on it. "This is for you."

He set down the oars, took the letter and examined it.

"Special delivery," she said, "from Tina Scott."

He got a wary look, and Alex suspected that he wanted to pitch the envelope into the lake.

"I think you'd better read it. When I take on an obligation, I like to see it through to completion."

Colin reluctantly tore open the envelope. He needed only a few seconds to scan the sheet of pale violet stationery inside. Looking pained now, he stuffed the sheet back into the envelope.

Alex's curiosity had returned full force. "I wouldn't expect you to tell me what it says, you know."

"But you'd like me to tell you."

"Tina already gave me the gist of it. You do have good taste in women, Colin. She's riveting."

"I don't have any complaints about her," he said diplomatically. "But the relationship was over a long time ago."

"Not for her."

"Alex, are you trying to set me up?"

She trailed her other hand in the water. "Not in the least. I already told Tina that I'm not involved in your personal life."

"In answer to your unspoken question—no, I was never in love with her. And, despite what she says, I doubt she was ever in love with me."

Alex didn't know why she felt relieved all of a sudden. "Five summers in a row, Colin. You can't blame the woman for harboring some hope."

He gave the envelope back to her and picked up the oars. "It didn't mean a whole lot to either of us."

Alex turned the envelope around in both hands. "You're not making a good case for yourself," she murmured. "Maybe it *should* have meant something. Colin...I wonder if you're not a whole lot like Tina when it comes to the opposite sex. I mean, she's always had more guys than she knows what to do with. Maybe you're the same way with women. Maybe they just flock to you, and in the process they become a devalued commodity."

"Lord," he said. "What have the two of you been talking about?"

"Prove me wrong, then. Tell me that women haven't been a plentiful resource."

"Resource," he muttered. "Commodity. Is this some new economic theory of interpersonal relations?"

She waited, and at last he spoke in a grudging tone.

"I've never thought of it that way before."

When he didn't say anything else, Alex couldn't help herself. "Was Beth one of the women who... flocked?"

"It's not like I snapped my fingers and she was there, Alex. And getting divorced sure as hell doesn't make you feel you can have any woman just for the asking.''

He might not admit it, but Alex knew there would always be plenty of women who would find Colin McIntyre a potent attraction. He wouldn't even need to snap his fingers. She examined the envelope one more time and held it out to him.

''I think you'd better keep this.''

''Why, Alex? You're the one I want.''

Now *she* nearly dropped the envelope in the lake. ''Colin, don't...''

''It's the truth. I want you. And maybe you feel the same way.''

Alex stared out over the water. She couldn't seem to speak.

''I know what you'll tell me,'' Colin went on. ''You'll tell me that not only are you still married technically, you have yet to savor your freedom as a divorcée. But those are only excuses, Alex.''

''Not to me.''

''The guy hurt you. And you think I'd do the same.''

''No.'' She clenched her hands in her lap. ''It's not that. I know you're not like Jonathan. You would never hurt anyone. Not physically or any other way—''

She stopped abruptly, but her words seemed to

leave an imprint on the air. After a long moment, Colin spoke.

"What are you saying, Alex? How exactly did this guy hurt you?"

She continued to stare out over the water, not looking at him. "It didn't get that far," she said, her voice tight. "He never…hit me, if that's what you're thinking. But there were signs that things could get worse. After all, when your husband tries to smash his fist through a wall, it's hard to ignore." She folded her arms against her body, but that didn't help dispel the coldness she still felt deep inside.

"You did the right thing," Colin said. "Getting away."

"Rationally, logically—I know that. But emotionally…"

Colin gazed at her. "You still haven't let go, have you? You really are still married to the guy."

She didn't know what to think. Ever since coming to Idaho, nothing was clear to her. Nothing at all.

"Colin…please. You asked me to spend the day with you. Can't we just do that? Spend this day together and not look any further ahead?"

He didn't answer at first. But then, at last, he nodded. "All right, Alex. We'll just take today."

IT WAS A GOOD DAY. That was Colin's assessment at the end of it. He and Alex had drifted the morning away on the lake. When they'd started to get hungry, they'd rowed to shore and then walked down the road to the small grocery-tackle store. They'd had to be inventive about lunch: pretzels, oranges, doughnuts, lime soda. After that they'd kept walking, making their way along the edge of the lake. When they'd finally returned to the house, they'd taken another tour of the place, and Alex had told him her suggestions for the decor.

The truth was, Colin hadn't thought about decor one way or another. He'd definitely bought the place on impulse. Denise down at Maggie's Diner had mentioned that Linda of Linda Wilcox Realty was shopping around a great lakeside property. On the spur of the moment, Colin had come to see the place. And known right away that he wanted it.

He wasn't in the habit of buying houses just for the heck of it. But this one had spoken to him. What it had said, among other things, was...*Alex*.

That was the part that had thrown him—that the house seemed as though it would fit Alex. Seemed the kind of place *she* could settle into. Which was not something that made a lot of sense. Especially since Alex was right about one thing: Colin wasn't known for settling down.

Now the sun was setting over the lake, the water

reflecting crimson and gold. Dinner was another impromptu meal, courtesy of Lakeside Pizza Delivery. They ate on the shore in front of the house, and that made for atmosphere hard to beat. As the air grew cool, he gathered branches and some logs from the wood bin beside the house. Soon he had a fire crackling on the sand.

He glanced at Alex. She sat a wary distance from the fire, her arms clamped around her knees, her face stiff. He cursed himself. How had he forgotten?

"I'll put it out," he said.

"No." Her answer had come too quickly. But then she took a deep breath. "No," she repeated more calmly. "This is ridiculous. I'm not going to let the damn thing get the better of me. It's just a...a campfire. Something that makes most people feel secure."

Colin sat beside her. "But even the sight of fire has you terrified. And there has to be a reason for that."

"Oh, I know—believe me." Her voice was brittle. "I've figured out quite a few things already. Something happened to me a long time ago in Montana. I don't know what it was...but I know that's where it happened. And I know that my mother is hiding the truth from me."

Colin studied her profile in the flickering firelight. Her chin was tilted just a little; her dark blond hair flowed back from her face. She looked vulnerable and combatant at once.

"I called," she went on, her voice carefully emotionless now. "I called my mother, and asked her flat out if anything had happened to me. She didn't try to lie, Colin. She tried as hard as she could *not* to lie. She said things like, 'Don't you think I'd tell you what you need to know?' and 'Why don't you trust me, Alex?' No outright denial, no false assurances. She's hiding something, all right."

"Ask her again."

"You'll have to talk to my mother sometime. Find out for yourself how good she is at not giving anything away. If she doesn't want to say something—she won't."

He thought about it. Human behavior was hardly his area of expertise, but an idea came to him.

"Ever been to a hypnotist, Alex?"

"Only as a student, of course," she said. "Part of psychology's basic training, so to speak."

"Maybe I'm just thinking of all those shows you see when you're a kid," he admitted. "The old guy in a waistcoat who swings his pocket watch in front of you. Or the guy who brings you up onstage and makes you do whatever he asks."

"Don't forget the hypnotist who conveniently

gets you to remember all your past lives.'' She
paused. ''Okay, I'm not really making fun. Under
the right conditions, the technique is valid. A couple of times, I've referred my own patients to hyp-
notherapists.''

''There you go,'' Colin said.

She scrambled to her feet and took a few steps
back, distancing herself even more from the fire.
''I said it was a valid technique under the right
conditions. That doesn't necessarily apply to *me*.''

''It was just an idea.''

''Dammit, Colin. I feel like I'm...like I'm un-
raveling. And I hate it. Don't you see? I hate it.''
Her voice shook.

Colin didn't have any more suggestions to give
her. So he went to her and took her into his arms,
instead.

She stood rigidly in his embrace. It occurred to
him that he'd never known a woman as complex
as Alex, as difficult to reach. She was fighting so
many battles—the ex-husband who wasn't as ex as
he should be, the many unknown fears. Trying to
do all that on her own had to be exhausting.

''Alex...let somebody help now and then.
Maybe even somebody like me.''

''What can you do for me, Colin?'' she whispered against his chest. ''How can you help me?''

"I don't know," he answered honestly. "Maybe just by being around."

"That's not the kind of rescue you're accustomed to making. And I keep telling you...I don't want to be rescued."

"So consider me a friend."

"A friend..."

At last she seemed to relent in his arms. She leaned against him, took whatever he could give her. He brushed his lips over her cheek. She was the one who turned her head, offering her mouth to him. She kissed him almost frantically, pressing herself to him, tracing his face with her hands. And then, abruptly, she pulled away.

"I don't...this isn't what I need, Colin. Not this kind of friendship." Bowing her head, she walked away from him, down the dark shore of the lake alone.

NEXT AFTERNOON, HERB'S living room looked like a computer store. One monitor sprouted from the coffee table, another from the end table. Colin stood in the doorway and saw processors, cables, keyboards, a couple of mouse pads. Sean and Herb were in the middle of it all.

"Mind telling me what's going on?" Colin asked.

Herb peered at one of the monitors as if it would

tell his fortune. "Your boy here says I need to become computer literate. I decided to take him up on it."

Colin's grandfather saying things like "computer literate." Somehow it just didn't seem right.

"This stuff must have cost you a fortune, Herb."

"The kid bought it. Pulled out his credit card and made a phone call."

Colin looked at his son. Sean was sprawled on his stomach, using a screwdriver on one of the processors.

"Sean, not a good idea—"

"What's the big deal? It's not like I can't afford it. And Grandpa Herbie really needs to get up to speed."

"About time I joined the electronic age," Herb announced.

Colin winced. It all sounded so reasonable. So worthy, even. Yet he still didn't like any of it.

"Sean, I don't know what kind of money you spend in California, but here it's different. Here you're on a budget."

"Why?"

"Kid's got a point," Herb said. "He makes his own money—no denying it."

Colin frowned at his grandfather. "What happened to the virtues of plugging away in a mine for rock-bottom wages?''

''The way I look at it,'' Herb said, ''Sean and I are similar. We both started out young, both had to learn how to handle the real world.''

''Television? You're calling that the real world?''

Sean went on tinkering with one of the cables, but he and Herb exchanged a conspiratorial glance. Things were really bad, Colin decided, when you felt you couldn't control either your grandfather or your son.

''So the boy makes a whole lot more money than I ever saw,'' Herb said. ''It's not like he's going out, spending it on extravagances. What's wrong with a couple of computers?''

''These aren't even the most expensive,'' Sean said. ''And you made it so Herbie and I have to spend all our time together. We gotta have something to do. What's the problem, Dad?''

The kid sounded so innocent. That was what bothered Colin most of all—Sean's concerted effort to appear the virtuous great-grandson.

For the moment, though, Colin couldn't think of a good objection. That bothered him, too.

THE OBJECTIONS CAME A DAY later. Colin walked into the house and found his grandfather rooted in front of a computer screen, his hands clamped around a small steering wheel.

"Where's Sean?" Colin asked.

"Hmmph…"

Herb jerked the wheel right, then left, his eyes glued to the monitor. Colin walked around behind him so he could see the monitor, too. He had to admit the racing simulation was impressive. You stared at the track whizzing along on the screen, and there was almost the sense you were strapped into a race car.

"Where's Sean?" Colin asked again.

"Huh?" Herb wheeled hard left. Lord. His own grandfather, a computer junkie. Colin leaned closer to him. "Herb."

"Don't distract me—damn, I crashed."

Herb let go of the wheel and punched a few keys, obviously getting ready to rev up again. Colin slid the keyboard away from him. "Herb, let's try this again. Where's Sean?"

Herb rubbed his hair. "I don't know. He's around here somewhere. Why wouldn't he be?"

Good question. Colin went through the rest of the house, looking for his son. Sean was nowhere to be seen.

Colin went back to the living room. Herb was at it again. This time Colin had to appropriate the steering wheel.

"What's the big idea?" Herb grumbled.

"Let me spell it out. Sean's not here."

Herb glanced around, as if expecting to see the boy materialize any second. "Can't be. The two of us have an understanding. He does what I tell him...I give him some slack."

"Apparently you gave him too much. Didn't you even notice him leave?"

Herb gazed sheepishly at the computer screen. "I've been a little involved."

That was an understatement. But Colin figured he only had himself to blame. He was the one who'd let Herb be in charge of Sean. He'd hoped it would ease the tension a little, and for a while it had seemed to work. Sean had been less sullen, less rebellious, these past few days. A couple of times he and Colin had even exchanged normal, ordinary, everyday remarks.

But none of that altered the fact that Sean had pulled the same old game all over again. Maybe he hadn't ditched Colin, but he'd ditched Herb.

And that meant no more slack.

ALEX SIPPED A CUP OF TEA at her seat in Maggie's Diner. Odd how she'd already established "her" booth. It was the one in the corner, away from the door, giving her a needed sense of privacy. Everyone in Sobriety already knew she was a psychologist. And that meant any hour of the day, she could expect perfect strangers to come up to her and ask for advice about problems with spouses and sisters and bosses and the neighbors next door. She'd hoped that getting away from Chicago would give her a break from all that. She'd been wrong.

Fortunately the only other patron in the restaurant at the moment was a teenage girl eating a pistachio sundae at the counter. But then the door opened, and Sean McIntyre came in.

The girl at the counter froze, staring at him raptly. He was wearing his dark glasses, and slunk past her.

"Hi, Sean," Alex said from her corner. "Want to join me?"

Despite the glasses, the relief on his face was unmistakable. He slid onto the seat across from her and slouched down. The girl at the counter gazed after him another moment, then reluctantly returned to her sundae.

Denise came drifting out of the kitchen, looked bored when she saw Sean and took his order for French fries and apple cobbler with chocolate ice cream. Sean removed the sunglasses.

"Having people recognize you, having them look at you all the time, stinks, doesn't it?" Alex remarked. "Sometimes, all you want is…not to be looked at."

Sean didn't say anything, just gave Alex a guarded glance. She'd already learned that he didn't talk much, at least not when she was around. No matter. She could carry the conversation herself.

"Last year I was on a talk show a couple of times. I didn't think it was going to be any big deal. I mean, pretty much all I'd done before that was write a few very obscure articles on the psychology of dating. I didn't count on the fact that dating is always a hot topic. Anyway, I got asked on this talk show in Chicago to talk about my specialty. Then I got asked back. Next thing I know, people are coming up to me on the streets, giving me that look…you know, the one that says just because people see you on TV, they think they know you, think they have a *right* to you."

Sean gave a quick, almost involuntary nod.

"Of course, it's nothing like being on a sitcom," Alex said. "Not that I'm complaining. Two appearances on the screen were enough. I don't know how you handle it, Sean. Having to deal with that all the time would drive me crazy."

Sean leaned his elbows on the table and stared out the window. "Everybody else tells me how great I have it."

"Maybe you do. Maybe I'm totally wrong."

He glanced down at the table now. "I didn't know how it was going to be. I thought it would be something…I thought I would be somebody…" He trailed off.

After another minute or so, Denise came with the French fries, the cobbler and the ice cream. She still looked bored as she slid the plates in front of Sean, even though everybody in town knew that Colin McIntyre's son was a celebrity. Then she wandered off again.

Alex sipped some more of her tea. "Have you noticed how we always figure that acquiring something is what will make us feel we're a somebody? I always thought getting a degree in psychology would make me feel legitimate."

Sean ate a French fry. "Did it work?"

"In a way—yes. When I got that degree it felt like such a big accomplishment. But after the excitement wore off…well, I realized I was still the same person. Nothing magical had happened to transform me."

Sean ate another French fry. "It was like that for me. At first I was really excited about being on TV. But now…" He looked unhappy, and for a few minutes he didn't touch the plate of fries.

"Now what, Sean?" Alex asked matter-of-factly.

"I don't feel like somebody. I feel like…nobody. I feel like…a failure."

She was careful not to show surprise. "The rest of the world thinks you're a great success."

He stared at the table again. "The work's hard," he said in a low voice. "Really hard. And you have to be really good at it. Only, I'm not. Sometimes I get so scared I forget my lines. And I get these nightmares where I screw everything up. And everybody gets mad at me…"

Alex knew about nightmares. She also knew that a fifteen-year-old boy shouldn't be having them.

"Who's everybody, Sean?"

"Everybody on the set. People try to be nice, but every time they look at me, I know they're thinking how stupid I am."

"Maybe they're scared, too. Everyone must be under a lot of pressure—trying to keep a show together…trying to keep it going."

"No…they all know what they're doing," Sean said flatly. "Nobody feels the way I do."

That was hardly likely, but Alex didn't contradict him. She knew that when you were feeling bad, everything looked bleak, and you had a hard time believing anyone else might be as insecure and uncertain as you.

"Don't tell my dad, all right? Don't tell him

anything I said.'' Sean sounded very intent all of a sudden.

Alex wrapped her hands around her teacup. ''If you don't want me to, of course I won't. But maybe you should talk to him yourself.''

''No.'' The single word was emphatic.

''Why not?''

''Because he never screws up.''

Now Alex did allow some surprise to show through. ''Your father doesn't try to put that kind of image across.''

''He never screws up,'' Sean repeated dourly. ''He saves people. And when you save people, you can't screw up.''

Alex didn't know if she could argue with that. But just then the subject of their conversation came through the door of the diner.

He walked toward Alex and Sean—and he didn't look pleased to see either one.

CHAPTER NINE

FATHER AND SON STARED at each other. Alex sipped some more tea. She figured even she might have flinched under Colin's steel-blue gaze, but Sean just scowled right back.

"Mind telling me," Colin said, "what you're doing here?"

Sean didn't answer. He did, however, deliberately eat a French fry. Alex saw the frustration in Colin's eyes. For once, she was genuinely glad not to be a parent.

"Well," she murmured, scooting to the edge of the seat, "I guess I'll be leaving..."

Sean gave her a look that stated, plain and clear, *Hey, don't go. Please.*

The last thing she wanted was to get caught in a confrontation between Colin McIntyre and his son. Any problems they had were their business, not hers. But then Colin glanced at her.

"Got room for me?" he asked.

She scooted to the far side of the bench. "Sure," she said lamely.

Colin slid in beside her. Now both of them were facing Sean...and Alex didn't have any avenue of escape.

Colin nodded at the apple cobbler and ice cream. "Seems nobody's going to eat that."

Sean gazed at the cobbler, too, then pushed it over toward his father.

Colin took a bite. "Not bad."

Given the hint of uncertainty in Sean's expression, he'd probably expected to be yelled at. But Colin wasn't doing any yelling. Instead he went on eating cobbler and ice cream.

"Guess you're still trying to prove a point," Colin told his son at last. "You got Herb hooked on the computer, then you just walked out on him."

"What's the big deal?" Sean muttered.

"The big deal is that Herb trusted you. I trusted you, too."

"You're the one trying to prove some stupid point. Why don't you just lock me up somewhere?"

There was something about teenagers, Alex reflected. One minute you felt sorry for them; the next they drove you nuts. At this particular moment, Alex wasn't feeling sympathetic. Colin, however, showed admirable restraint. He finished the dessert, and only then did he speak.

"Hmm, lock you up somewhere. Interesting idea. But I have one that's even better."

Sean looked suspicious. "What?"

"You'll see," Colin said enigmatically. "It isn't a bad idea…not a bad idea at all."

Now Sean looked uneasy. Meanwhile, Colin had the embattled appearance of someone who'd won the first round but wasn't at all sure about the second.

Alex couldn't say she envied him.

COLIN WISHED HE'D THOUGHT of something like this sooner. It was just what he and Sean needed: a whole weekend off backpacking together, just the two of them. No distractions…no grandfather. And no pretty psychologist who seemed to get along better with his son than he did.

The sun was barely up as Colin finished stowing their gear. He went to the kitchen, opened the freezer and took out the plastic bottles he'd tossed in there last night. In a couple of hours the ice in the bottles would melt, providing refreshing cold water on the trail. Nothing like a cold drink after you'd been hiking for a while, Colin knew, and smiled to himself.

A knock sounded at the front door. Dusty trotted down the hall, sat down in front of the door and barked.

"All right, all right, I'll get it," Colin told him. "But who'd be here this early…"

He opened the door and found out. Alex stood on the front porch, prettier than ever. She wore a khaki shirt, hiking shorts that bristled with pockets, thick hiking socks and hiking boots. A backpack with a sleeping bag attached was slung over her shoulders. Everything had that brand-new, unused look.

"Let me guess," Colin said. "You just happened to be out for a stroll."

"Very funny. I'm here for our outing, of course."

"Our outing," he repeated.

"Right."

Obviously this wasn't going anywhere. Colin came out onto the porch, closing the door behind him. The dog, however, managed to squeeze through and bounded over to Alex. She bent and gave him a pet.

"Hello there, Dusty. At least you're glad to see me."

"I'm always glad to see you, Alex," Colin said. "Thought you'd figured that out by now."

She straightened. "You're only glad to see me when it's on *your* terms. And right now…it's not on your terms. But here's the deal. Your son called me yesterday and asked me to come on this backpacking trip. No, 'ask' isn't the right word—he practically begged me. Believe me, at first I said no. Spending two days in the wilderness with the McIntyre males isn't the most tantalizing prospect in the world. But Sean can be persuasive, and he said you wanted me to come. I wasn't entirely convinced of *that,* but I thought at least he would have told you about the invite by now.'' She paused, a little out of breath. ''Have I answered all your questions?''

''Not by a long shot.'' He looked her over. ''Why'd you really decide to tag along, Alex?''

She didn't seem pleased with his choice of words. ''I told you—your son can be persuasive. He said he didn't know what he'd do alone with you for two whole days. He said he wanted an intermediary.''

''Lord. That's the word he used?''

''The exact one,'' said Alex.

Colin wondered what the hell was up with his son. ''Why doesn't the kid just hire a lawyer and be done with it? He thinks he can't talk to me without a damn…a damn *intermediary?*''

''So he has a bit of a melodramatic streak.''

Colin pushed a hand through his hair. ''I try to talk to my son, Alex. Believe me, I try.''

''I know you do,'' Alex said. She sounded sympathetic.

"So you came along out of the goodness of your own heart," he grumbled.

"Partly. But there's another reason I decided to." She folded her arms and looked at him almost defiantly. "Colin, I've gotten off track in Idaho. I flew all the way out here so I could research you. As I'm sure you've noticed, not a whole lot of researching has gone on. It's time to rectify that."

He glanced dubiously at her backpack. "Don't tell me—you've got your tape recorder in there."

"Of course not. But here's what I figure. Two days in the wild with you and I can't help but do some research. It should be pretty painless for you. What do you say?"

He perused Alex. She didn't have that strained expression today—the one that said she'd had that nightmare. Instead she appeared determined and energetic. He could view the interview as a distraction for her.

The door opened behind him, and Sean came out. He ducked down to pet Dusty, then slowly straightened.

"I'm ready," he said, his gaze darting between Colin and Alex. He looked a little defiant, a little sheepish.

Colin knew he could play the heavy. He could drag his son off into the wilderness and try to force some family togetherness. Or he could give in and take along the...intermediary.

"Okay," he said. "Let's hit the trail."

ALEX CLEARLY WASN'T ONE of those people who complained on a hike. She kept up a good pace, and she stopped only now and then for a water break. But after they'd been hiking a couple of hours, Colin saw that she was favoring her left foot. He called a halt.

"We made a pit stop a couple of minutes ago," Alex said. "I'm going on."

"Take off your shoe. And your sock."

She gave him an exasperated glance, but she sat down on a boulder and started unlacing her boot. Sean hiked farther up the trail, pointedly out of hearing range. But Colin could see him slip off his pack and perch on a boulder of his own. He seemed lost in his thoughts. If he didn't appear relaxed, at least the resentful, unhappy expression he so often wore had disappeared. Colin supposed he could be grateful for any small sign of progress.

"Ready for inspection," Alex said, sticking her foot out.

"Nice toes," he said. But, just as he had suspected, a good-size blister was forming on her heel.

"Ever been hiking before?"

"Of course," she answered. "Maybe it's been a while, that's all."

"Must have been a long while. What'd you do, buy out all of Steve's Outfitters?" He picked up her boot and inspected it. "Too stiff. Someone should have warned you. You need to break these in first. They're rubbing your heels, and that's why you're getting blisters."

"Blister," she amended. "I'll tighten the laces and then I'll be fine. I'm not going to hold us back."

"This isn't a forced march." He reached into his pack and brought out a small first-aid kit.

"You're prepared for everything, aren't you?" said Alex.

"Even blisters." He took out a bandage and put it on her heel. "Other one," he said.

She muttered, but she removed the other shoe and sock.

No blister yet, he noted, but he supplied a bandage as a preventative. When she put her socks and boots back on, he knelt in front of her and began doing up the laces.

"Colin, I really can do this myself."

He glanced up at her. "You're not willing to take any help from me?"

"Okay…you do the laces."

He finished, then had her walk a little to test them.

"No heel slippage," she said in a tone of satisfaction. "I'm ready to go again."

The three of them went on. It seemed important to Alex to prove she could keep up with the guys. Pines jutted up all around. The trail itself was packed thick with decayed leaves and pine needles, pleasingly spongy beneath Colin's feet. The air was as clean and sharp as only mountain air can be. He felt some long-held tension leave his body. It had been way too long since he'd been backpacking. He always intended to go with Sean...but until now Sean just hadn't appeared interested.

At the moment Sean and Alex were walking a little ahead. Their voices floated back to Colin. Alex was describing a girlhood camping trip she'd taken, and now and then Sean made comments about a trip he'd taken with a couple of friends about a year ago.

Colin drew his eyebrows together, his good mood all too fleeting. This was the first *he'd* heard about Sean's camping trip. Apparently the kid liked the outdoors well enough. So why had he avoided father-son camping trips?

Alex fell back into step beside Colin. Her cheeks were flushed from exertion and from the cool air. She'd pulled her hair back under a bandanna, but several golden strands had escaped. She kept trying to tuck them back into place, but finally she gave up.

"Colin...I'm having a good time. I hope I'm not the only one."

"Is this part of being an intermediary?" he asked. Sean had gone on ahead again, and there wasn't much danger of him overhearing. Nonetheless, Alex answered in a low voice.

"I wish you knew what Sean was really thinking. If only he'd *talk* to you—"

"I take it he's talked to you...maybe more than I'd realized. The two of you did seem pretty intent at the diner the other day."

Alex sighed. "He asked me not to tell you what we discussed."

"Patient-doctor privilege?"

"I'm not your son's *shrink,* for goodness' sake. He just happened to tell me a few things. Colin, they're things you need to hear, but not from me. Somehow you've got to get through to him."

"Any suggestions? I'm open, believe me."

Now she looked regretful. "I'm sorry, Colin. Sorry I'm not more help with your son."

She was more help than she knew. At least the kid was talking to somebody.

Colin resented only one fact: his son wasn't talking to *him.*

THAT NIGHT, WHEN SEAN wanted to start a camp-fire, Colin studied Alex, ready to nix the idea. She returned his gaze tranquilly.

"Sounds fine to me."

This time she actually sat close to the fire. Try as he might, Colin saw no fear in her expression.

After dinner they toasted marshmallows and sat around the fire. Alex and Sean talked about nothing in particular, then Alex and Colin talked about nothing in particular. The Colin and Sean combi-nation didn't work so well, since Sean answered Colin's attempts at conversation in monosyllables. Alex tried to get a three-way communication go-ing, and that was slightly more successful. Maybe she'd have to stick around permanently as the McIntyre family go-between.

Colin was thinking he might like Alex to stick around, but the prospect seemed remote under the starlit night. He stared into the fire, searching for answers.

Alex started some silly game that had to do with her and Sean making up ghost stories. She even got the kid to laugh once. After a while Sean stretched out in his sleeping bag, and he gazed into the fire, too. The next time Colin glanced at him, he saw that his son was sound asleep.

"When he was little," Colin murmured, "Beth and I got a kick out of watching him sleep. One or the other of us would be strung out from taking care of him all day, but we'd forget the irritations as soon as he hit the pillow. We'd look at him, and think how lucky we were.''

"Not much has changed, has it?" Alex murmured back.

He almost smiled. "Not much. Except that back then I actually had a relationship with my son."

"He's lucky to have a father like you. He'll figure that out, sooner or later."

"Right." Colin didn't have much faith.

Alex moved closer to him. "Thanks for letting me come along. I really am having a good time."

He put his arm around her, drew her closer. "Forget me 'letting' you come. You bulldozed your way in—remember?"

"I suppose I did." She didn't sound repentant.

They went on sitting there together, warmed by the fire. Sean moved restlessly in his sleep, then settled down again. Colin supposed he should just be grateful for this moment. They'd created the illusion of a family outing, and he had a beautiful woman next to him...a woman who for once did not seem chased by the shadows in her life. Maybe it was wrong to want more.

He wanted more anyway.

ALEX FOUND NO DREAMS in these mountains...no nightmares, either. She felt almost at home, tucked into her sleeping bag, knowing that Colin was close by. She slept deeply, peacefully. Once only did she wake, opening her eyes to gaze at where the fire had left nothing but embers. She marveled at the fact that her nameless terror seemed to have vanished. It was as if someone had cut the chains binding her. For this moment, at least, she was free. She fell asleep again, drifting gratefully into the dreamless night.

When she awoke in the morning, sunlight spilled upon her, reaching her through the pines. She sat up, stretching, and looked around for Colin and Sean. Their sleeping bags were empty.

For a short while, she didn't think anything of it, just took it as a good sign: father and son off together somewhere. Maybe they'd finally get a little rapport going. She climbed out of her sleeping bag and found her toothbrush. Then, realizing that she was starving, she opened a package of granola, sat cross-legged on her sleeping bag and started munching.

The forest was very quiet. There were birds, of course, but Alex heard no other sounds. She suddenly felt very alone. With a little shiver, she remembered last night's ghost stories. They could easily have included waking up alone in your sleeping bag, with everyone else vanished...

"Don't be stupid," she chided herself. She'd been awake for less than ten minutes. What was wrong with her now?

Then she did hear a sound—someone shouting through the woods. Colin—calling, "Sean."

Alex stood up. Only a few seconds later, Colin came striding toward her through the pines. His expression was grim.

"What's wrong?" she asked, her heartbeat speeding up. "What's happened?"

"You haven't seen him?" Colin asked brusquely.

"No. I woke up, and both of you were gone. Colin, what's happened?"

"When I woke up, he was already gone. Looks like he's run away again." Colin swore, then swung on his pack and started buckling it.

She stared at Sean's empty sleeping bag. "It doesn't make any sense. Where would he run to?"

"God only knows. The kid's trying damn hard to prove he doesn't need me. Maybe that's okay in town, where he can whip out his credit card and hire a limo. But out here..." He didn't say anything more.

Alex grabbed her socks and boots. "Surely he'd stick to the trail...wouldn't he? He's probably up ahead just a little."

"We can hope. I don't even know how good a

head start he has. Could be a couple of hours—could be more. You stay here, Alex. I'm going to look for him.''

''No.'' She laced her boots clumsily. ''I'm coming with you. It's better if we stick together.''

CHAPTER TEN

EARLY THAT AFTERNOON, Colin found evidence that Sean had left the trail. It wasn't anything Alex would have noticed at first, just some small rocks that had been disturbed at the side of the trail and an indentation in the ground that could have been made by the toe of a boot.

"It's possible he went this way," Colin said.

"Are you sure?"

He glanced at her dourly. "I'm not sure of anything, Alex. It's been guesswork the whole time. Maybe he left the trail hours ago. Maybe not. But looks like there's an outcrop up there—exactly the kind of place where I'd choose to rest."

Alex clambered up the slope behind Colin. The boy was stretched out on the promontory, fast asleep. Alex nudged him awake, and Sean sat up with a start.

"What the hell—"

"My question precisely," said Colin.

Alex saw his jaw clench, as unmistakable anger quickly replaced unmistakable relief. Then, without another word, he turned and walked away. A moment later he disappeared from view.

Sean gazed after him. "Where's *he* going?" he muttered.

Alex sat down on the rock next to the boy. She felt light-headed with her own relief. "I imagine your father wants to pummel you," she said, almost conversationally. "And, being the man he is, he's probably absenting himself until he can get hold of his anger. Sean, I've had some experience with a man who *couldn't* control his temper. You should be glad your father's not like that. By the way, I have the urge to pummel you myself. Why did you do it?"

Sean looked both defensive and guilty. "Who cares."

Alex eased off her pack, took out one of her water bottles and treated herself to a long drink. "Why'd you do it?" she repeated.

"I don't know," he mumbled.

"Cut the bull."

"I just had to get away—all right?"

"No," Alex said. "It's damn well not all right. My guess is you almost started to have a good time yesterday. You almost felt safe and protected— your father can make people feel like that. You started to feel so safe and protected it scared you.

Heaven forbid you should need your own father. So you ran away."

"I wasn't running away. I was *getting* away."

"Same difference," Alex said.

The boy didn't say anything else. He just sat there looking unhappy and defiant. But he was unharmed. Maybe, right now, that was all that mattered.

NEXT MORNING, a large envelope arrived by courier from Alex's office in Chicago. She took it up to her room at the bed-and-breakfast, then sat down and stared at it. She didn't need to open it—she already knew what was inside.

At last, however, she tore open the package and extracted the sheaf of documents.

Her divorce papers. She was no longer a married woman.

She thumbed through the pages, even though she already knew what they said. The lawyers had worked everything out. She and Jonathan would sell the house, split the proceeds. Other possessions would be disposed of fairly and equitably. Despite Jonathan's constant delays and quibblings, it was all over now.

Alex set down the papers. She felt numb. *Divorced*—she tried the word out, but it didn't have the meaning that she'd hoped. She didn't feel free—she just felt empty.

She went over to the desk, opened her laptop and turned it on. She tried to get some work done, but she was only going through the motions. She stared at the words on the screen—words about Colin McIntyre, rescuer.

Gradually, as she sat there, the numbness lifted. She was not grateful, however. The intense emotions that assaulted her now were overwhelming. She pressed her hands to her cheeks, as if that would somehow calm the tumult of her heart.

Suddenly, she understood clearly what she had to do next.

HERB WAS IN THE ATTIC, looking for ghost clothes.

Colin hadn't thought it could get any worse… but apparently it could. Herb had decided that when it came to hauntings, a plain white sheet was simply too uninspired. To his reasoning, a miner's ghost would wear something more rugged: vintage overalls, for instance.

Colin stooped down as he walked across the dusty floorboards. Herb sat on a stool, rummaging through a trunk of old odds and ends.

"Look at this," he told Colin, holding up a 1940s-style hat in brown felt. The crown was a little lopsided, but otherwise the hat was in good condition. "Belonged to my dad…your great-grandpa. Wore it every Sunday I can remember."

"Do you save everything, Herb?"

"Just about," said his grandfather imperturbably. He gave Colin an astute glance. "Still smarting about the way your camping trip backfired?"

The old man did have a way of getting right to the point. Colin sat down on another trunk. "Seemed like a good idea at the time."

"If you'd asked me—which nobody did—I'd have told you right off it was just an invitation for the kid to act up again. Damn lucky you found him on that mountain."

Damn lucky, indeed.

"You surprised me," Herb said, "not grounding the kid again."

"It didn't do any good last time. I'm trying to think of something better." No ideas so far. Today Sean's punishment was to spend the afternoon at the mining museum, helping Lillian catalog a donation of ore samples. Colin was trusting his son to be there when he went to pick him up in an hour. Was even that too much to expect?

"You know," Herb said, "I used to have a lot of trouble with your dad. He was always testing my authority…just like you did when you were a kid."

Colin wondered if he'd heard right. It was uncharacteristic of Herb to say anything even re-motely critical about Thomas.

"Don't know what it was," Herb said, "but he had to question everything. Sometimes I called it spirit. Sometimes I called it just plain cussedness."

"You're telling me Thomas drove you crazy sometimes?"

"Of course he did," Herb grumbled. "When did I ever say otherwise?"

"All the time, Herb. My entire life, you've made it sound like Dad was perfect."

"Oh, he shone, all right. Drew people to him, and he didn't even have to try. It's like people knew that if they were around him, something spe-cial would happen sooner or later. You just had to wait a little, that was all. The basketball court, for example. Your dad would be fooling around, not putting much into the game, making the coach mad...but at the last minute he'd pull off a free throw, and the team would win because of him. You'd realize that the wait, the suspense, had been worth it."

Herb truly was slipping. "He almost sounds like a real person," Colin said. "Somebody who screws up but who manages to come through in the end."

"I didn't say he screwed up. He was just a little overconfident sometimes. He was good and he knew it, so he figured he could afford to push things to the edge.''

Colin liked his version better. ''Everybody makes mistakes. Thomas had to have made a few.''

''I never painted him as perfect. Now, get off of there,'' Herb said, motioning Colin away from the trunk. ''I have some things to show you.'' Colin stood, allowing Herb to open the trunk. The old man brought out Thomas's high school yearbook. ''Seen this, haven't you? And this...'' Herb brought out more. The photo album of Thomas's earliest years. The ashtray he'd made in elementary school, the one Herb had used before Colin's grandmother made him give up smoking... Other items; other memories, so many of them. Herb was good at saving memories. The surprise was that he hadn't kept Thomas's room downstairs intact as a sort of shrine.

Now Herb was bending over the trunk, clutching something, a look of sorrow on his face.

''What is it, Herb—''

''Nothing.'' The old man dropped whatever he was holding and closed the trunk lid. ''Nothing,'' he repeated heavily. ''I've had enough for now. Let's get out of here.''

No question. Colin knew it was time to leave the memories behind. But something in that old trunk had disturbed his grandfather. And Colin couldn't help wondering what it was.

ALEX PACKED THE LAST of her things and snapped her suitcase shut. She glanced around her room at the bed-and-breakfast to see if she'd missed anything. No, she was ready to go.

She carried the suitcase down to her rental car and hoisted it into the trunk. But somehow she couldn't get into the car just yet. She had absolutely no doubt she was making the right decision, nevertheless she felt sad. She'd been in this little town such a short time, yet it tugged at her, telling her not to go.

A car pulled to a stop on the street. Alex turned—and could hardly believe who she saw.

"Hello, Alex."

All she could do was stare. "What are you doing here, Jonathan—how did you find me?"

"Lauren's my friend, too, remember. She thought maybe you'd want to see me."

Alex made a mental note to tell Lauren to be more discreet. However, how friends divided their loyalties after you got divorced was one of the stickier aspects of any split.

She studied her ex-husband. His sand-colored hair was mussed and he had a day's growth of beard. Not that it detracted from his appearance; he'd always carried off the scruffy look.

"What do you want?" Alex asked.

"To see you…that's all." He stepped toward her, and instinctively she took a step back.

"Alex, things are different now. I'm…I'm getting some help." He gave her the smile that had once charmed her. "I used to be married to a psychologist—now I'm consulting one. How's that for a switch?"

"I'm glad for you, Jonathan. But I still don't understand why you're here."

"I miss you. And I realize I botched a lot of things between us. Getting those papers hit me in the gut, Alex. Didn't you feel the same way?"

She wondered if this was really happening… Her ex-husband tracking her all the way to Idaho to say that he missed her.

"The end of our marriage hit me a long time ago," she said quietly.

"Alex…maybe I just came to say I'm sorry."

He sounded so reasonable, so sincere. But he'd sounded that way before. In the past he would give in to his anger and then he'd be sorry afterward— like someone who'd had too much to drink and who swore not to overindulge the next time, but always did.

"Look," she said. "It's over. We've both

known that for a long time. The papers just made it official.''

"Dammit, Alex—don't you feel anything?''

Oddly enough, she didn't...not where he was concerned. Seeing those divorce papers had made her realize that she'd moved beyond him, once and for all.

"Jonathan...go back to Chicago.''

He laughed harshly. "That's all you have to say, after the way I flew out here, then drove to this godforsaken place—''

"It's a nice place, actually. And you shouldn't have come.''

How quickly it happened—the anger darkening his expression. It was something ugly and repellent. And, she acknowledged with an odd detachment, it was something monotonous. She was tired of it.

"Go home, Jonathan. You don't belong here.''

The rest happened quickly, too—and so unexpectedly that at first she didn't have time to react. He took another step toward her and gripped her arm. His fingers dug painfully into her flesh. She tried to pull away, but his grip only tightened.

"Let me go,'' she said, as calmly as possible.

"I loved you,'' he said. "And you were so damn cold in return. You're still cold. Why, Alex? *Why?*''

He shook her. All she wanted was to get away from him. She struggled, but his hand was clamped around her arm. She stared into his face. She remembered something now… She remembered being a child and feeling this same terrible fear. And a terrible helplessness, too. She couldn't get away, no matter how hard she tried—

A car door slammed and footsteps came toward her. And then, blessedly, she heard Colin's voice.

"Let her go."

Jonathan gripped her arm all the more mercilessly. "You've already started something new, Alex? Damn you—"

Suddenly, Jonathan gave a grunt of surprise, then released her. She saw Colin lead him roughly away. Alex put her hands to her cheeks and felt tears there…and she realized they were the same kind of tears she'd cried in her nightmare.

"HOW DID YOU KNOW TO COME just then?" Alex said. "You're a rescuer, Colin, but still…"

"Tina called. She told me you were packing to leave. Funny, she just thought I'd like to know."

Alex smiled shakily. "I don't get it. What's she up to?"

"How's the arm?" Colin asked.

"Better." She rubbed it and looked out the window at the sun setting over the lake. Colin had brought her to his lakefront house after he'd dispensed with Jonathan.

"I don't know if I said thank you, Colin...but thank you."

"Here, let me see." He walked over to her and examined her arm. "You're going to have one hell of a bruise."

"Thank God that's all." She drew a deep breath. "Believe me, Colin, he never did anything physical like that before. He was emotionally abusive, of course. But he never crossed the line. Till today..."

"You're well rid of him," Colin said.

She gazed into his eyes. "I'm just glad the divorce papers finally came through. I guess I didn't tell you that, did I? I'm now a divorcée."

"So why were you all set to leave, Alex? Weren't you even going to say goodbye?"

"Yes...no...I don't know." She felt emotionally exhausted, and she went to settle down at the window seat. "When I saw those divorce papers, I knew I *had* to go. Because I no longer had enough excuses where you're concerned..."

He came to sit beside her and took her hand in his. So strong a man, so gentle a touch. She was grateful for gentleness just then.

"You need excuses where I'm concerned, Alex?"

"Apparently so. You don't know how confused I am right now. Colin, when Jonathan took hold of me, the strangest thing happened. I remembered something…something from long ago. Someone else holding me, and hurting me. And I felt that damn helplessness again, the kind I always feel in the nightmare." She shook her head wearily. "Everything's so jumbled. And right now I almost despise myself. How could I ever have cared for someone like Jonathan? All the excuses I made for him over the years, the way I stuck with him, the way I let him make me feel guilty for *his* failings— What was wrong with me?"

"You don't have to do this right now, Alex."

He kissed her gently, so very gently, just the way she needed. His finger traced a path over her cheek. When he halted, she shook her head.

"Don't stop," she whispered.

"You're not going to run away from me again?"

"Not tonight, anyway," she said in a low voice.

CHAPTER ELEVEN

COLIN HADN'T BEEN PREPARED for a night with Alex. The lake house had no furniture...no bedding. He had to improvise: a blanket from the Jeep spread out on the living room floor, a single candle flickering on the mantelpiece because the electricity wasn't yet turned on.

He and Alex sat on the blanket, facing each other rather formally. Alex drew her knees up and clasped her arms around them.

"Colin, about protection..." she said awkwardly.

"I don't have anything on me," he said, regretful. "I didn't plan this, you know."

"Yes, well..." She was having a difficult time with the subject, but she pushed on. "The fact is, I never went off the pill, so birth control isn't an issue. It's just that..."

"I'm okay," he said. "I'm always very careful, Alex—more than careful."

"I'm okay, too, so that's taken care of... Oh, damn. This feels like a business meeting." She sounded exasperated. "Where do we go from here?"

"Any other items you want to discuss?" he asked gravely.

"Meeting adjourned." Now her voice was barely above a whisper.

He moved closer to her. Together they lay down on the blanket. He could see her only dimly in the candlelight, but she pervaded his senses. Very slowly, she began to unbutton her shirt. She wore a camisole underneath, and he helped her with that. At last, her skin was bare and he could touch her. He heard the intake of her breath, and knew they both wanted more.

The undressing was a venture all in itself, something not to be rushed. His shirt, his jeans...her jeans, underwear—discarded, more hurriedly now. Then Alex's body next to his with nothing hidden, nothing denied.

He kissed her and touched her, and kissed her some more. At first she responded eagerly, openly. But then, suddenly, he felt her hesitation.

"We have all night," he murmured against her cheek.

She twined her hands in his hair. "Colin, it's the first time since...well, since..."

"Since your divorce?" he asked, his tone sober.

"I figured as much, since you've only been divorced—what is it, some twenty-four hours?"

"It's not a joke. I never should have jumped into bed with you so soon—"

"Technically we're not in bed, so it's all right." Some distraction was in order, so he brushed his lips over the swell of her breasts. He felt her tremble.

"Colin, what I'm trying to say is…this is embarrassing, but my husband—my *ex*-husband—is the only other man I've ever…" She didn't say anything more, and she didn't need to.

Now he ran his mouth over the curve of her shoulder. He could tell he was getting the response he wanted, but apparently she still had something on her mind.

"Colin, toward the end he kept saying I was *cold*. And he said it again today—"

"Trust me, Alex, you're not cold. You're warm and passionate. Don't you think I could tell that the first time I took you in my arms?"

"But—"

"Don't listen to anyone but me," he said. "Trust me."

He wasn't sure he'd gotten through to her. Maybe there was only one way to go about this: show her. So he kissed her again, making a path from her throat to her navel, and then beyond.

Alex arched against him, her breath coming raggedly, showing him in every way but words that she needed him. And then she opened herself to him, and neither of them held anything back. He heard her moan, heard her call his name, and together they tumbled over the edge into pure sensation.

Afterward, she lay sprawled next to him, her breath still coming unevenly, and he smiled.

"I think I just proved my point," he said.

"What?" she asked cautiously.

"That you're not a cold woman in the least. In fact, you're hot."

"Colin…"

She sounded embarrassed, but she also sounded like she wanted to hear more. So he told her…but not in words.

IF YOU LIVED IN SOBRIETY and you needed the amenities of a larger town, you went to Silver Lake. But if even Silver Lake couldn't meet your needs, you crossed the state line into Washington and you headed for Spokane. That was where Colin and Alex were heading right now.

Colin drove, glancing over at Alex every now and then. In the light of morning, she was reserved, quiet. Nothing like last night. At the lake house, in his arms, she'd been anything but.

"It's okay that we made love," he told her.

She winced. "Colin—"

"What do you want me to say, Alex—we had sex?"

She sighed. "I can't believe we actually did it. I mean, I've been a divorcée less than two days—"

"The way I see it, you should have been a divorcée a long time ago."

Alex looked prettier than ever today, her blond hair catching the sunshine; her skin seemed to glow. Colin figured that making love had agreed with her. It had agreed with him, too. He felt terrific.

"Colin, if you don't keep your eyes on the road, we'll be in trouble."

"We're already in trouble. Because if you're thinking what I'm thinking..."

She flushed. "I'm not thinking that at all," she said sternly. But when he reached over and clasped her hand, she curled her fingers around his.

After a moment, she spoke again. "I guess what I'm wondering is...well, you've had a lot of experience with women, haven't you?"

"Not as much as you think."

"Just tell me the truth," she said.

"Yes, I have been with...several women. And if you want to know how you compare, Alex—there is no comparison."

"What do you mean?"

"You're the best," he said.

"I don't believe you."

"Believe me." He smiled. He was telling the truth, all right.

She fell deep into thought, as if pondering his words. If she didn't believe him now, they'd just have to work it out later. He smiled some more. Then she drew her hand away, and he was sorry for that.

"Where do we go from here?" she asked.

Colin hadn't thought much beyond last night— and more nights exactly like it. He knew his life was still unsettled. He'd just bought a house in Idaho, but he hadn't decided if he was going to leave his job in California. Meanwhile, Alex lived in Chicago.

"We'll do it one step at a time," he told her.

"I wish we could. But I don't even know how to take the first step! Not with so much hanging over me. So much unanswered."

"Maybe today you'll get some answers." He was taking her to Spokane to see a hypnotist— correction, hypnotherapist, as she called it.

She'd had another nightmare last night. They'd made love once, then again...and then, at last, sated, they'd fallen asleep, tangled together. But only a short time later Colin had heard a distressed

sound from Alex as she dreamed. When he'd
gently awakened her, she'd been disoriented...and,
yes, terrified.

Earlier this morning he'd made a few calls,
found out who came recommended in the hypno-
therapy business and set up an appointment for her.
She hadn't objected. At this point, she was willing
to give anything a try.

"Scared?" he asked now.

"Yes," she said, holding her arms close to her
body and staring out the window. "What scares
me the most is that maybe this will work and I'll
find out something I don't want to know."

"You have to find the truth."

"I think the truth is starting to find me," she
said, "whether I want it or not."

THE HYPNOTHERAPIST, IRENE, was a woman of
about fifty or so, who looked like a business ex-
ecutive. She sat down with both Colin and Alex in
her office, and made it seem that talking about
nightmares and repressed memories was the most
reasonable thing in the world to do.

"As I'm sure you realize, Dr. Robbins, I can't
make you any promises about what you'll remember under my guidance. Because that's all hypnosis
is—a sort of guidance. You must do the work."

"Please call me Alex. And I'm ready for whatever happens...or doesn't."

Alex seemed nervous, but she also had the determined look that Colin was coming to know. She glanced at him as he rose to leave.

"Stay, Colin...please."

"If Alex wants you here, I think it would be best," said Irene. "Anything that will help her to relax more deeply."

Colin sat down again. The hypnosis procedure was surprisingly mundane. Irene had Alex stretch out on a reclining chair, then she lowered the blinds. She had Alex close her eyes, then she led her through some relaxation exercises, nothing more. Colin himself, seated a short distance from Alex, began to feel pleasantly sleepy. Then Irene talked about how she was going to count backward from ten, and after that Alex would go back into her childhood.

In the movies, the person being hypnotized would start to talk like a zombie. That had always struck Colin as hokey. But nothing of the kind happened here. The answers Alex gave to Irene's questions were guarded, and spoken very much in her normal voice. Yes, she believed she could remember being twelve...eleven...nine...six...

"No!" Alex cried suddenly, sitting upright with

a jerk. She was shaking. Colin went to her, took her hands in his.

"What happened, Alex?" Irene asked calmly.

"I don't know." Alex gripped Colin's hands. "I honestly don't know. It's just…I was so frightened again. I felt something—or someone—looming over me. And then the fire. Just like in my nightmare—the fire."

"So someone was there with you."

"No…*yes*. Some kind of presence. I couldn't see…" Her voice dropped. "I'm sorry. I can't do this anymore."

"That's fine. We've already made some progress." Irene raised the blinds again, as if to restore the ordinariness of the day. But Alex looked pale, her eyes shadowed, as if she did not believe life could ever be ordinary again.

"Alex," said Irene, "you might want to come back for another session. But I think you need to do something else, too. You need to talk to anyone in your family who might have knowledge of what you experienced."

Alex shook her head. "There's only my mother. And she *won't* talk. I've already tried."

"Perhaps you should try again," Irene said. "There's only so much we can do here, Alex. It seems you suffered a serious trauma in your childhood, and I believe you're going to need all the resources you can find.''

It wasn't the most reassuring answer in the world, but at least it was an honest one. As they left Irene's office, Alex was silent, and she was still quiet as they climbed into the Jeep. They sat there for a long moment. Finally Colin reached out to her once more. But this time, when he touched her, she flinched. He drew his hand away.

"I'm sorry," she said in a low voice. "I guess I'm a little frazzled."

Unfortunately, he knew it was more than that. "There's still something about me that scares you, Alex. That's the part that doesn't seem right."

"Dammit, none of it seems right! I'm more confused now than when I went into that office. Sometimes I wish…"

She didn't finish, so he did it for her.

"Sometimes you wish you'd never seen that video of me. And that you'd never come to Idaho."

She didn't deny it, just sat mutely and stared out the window. And he knew that despite what had happened between them last night, he and Alex were further apart than ever.

COLIN SURVEYED THE ITEMS spread in front of him on the dining room table: three credit cards, one bank card, some crumpled twenties and a fifty. Then he surveyed Sean. His son stood across from him, arms folded, expression ticked.

"You can't take any of them. They're mine."

"Let's just say I'm 'holding' them for you."

Sean scowled. "The hell you are."

Colin stacked the credit cards and bank card. "Grounding you didn't work. Confiscation is the next choice."

"The hell it is."

Colin almost felt sorry for the kid. A few minutes ago, Sean had emptied his wallet to demonstrate how financially independent he was. Whereupon Colin had appropriated the wallet's contents. He'd been thinking about a move like this for a day or so: take away the accoutrements of adulthood, and you might just get to the kid underneath.

"Here's the deal," Colin said. "The rest of the time you're here you get an allowance—like any normal fifteen-year-old."

"Yeah, well, I'm not normal."

Colin leaned back in his chair. "I think you are. At least, I think you want to be. Why not try it out? Being here's the perfect chance."

Sean seemed to hesitate, but then he glared at Colin again. "It's my money. I earned it."

"Doing something you hate."

"I don't hate it."

"You like it?"

Sean shrugged. "Yeah," he muttered.

"It's only a television show," Colin said.

Sean stiffened. "It matters. Even if I'm not saving people's lives."

The remark caught Colin by surprise. He hadn't meant to belittle the kid's job—and this was the first time Sean had ever expressed anything but contempt for Colin.

"I'm not saying that what you do, Sean, isn't important. If it makes you happy, it's important—to you and to me. But if it makes you miserable, it's okay if you want to walk away from it."

"Walk away—no thanks. I already feel like too much of a failure as it is."

Colin gazed at his son. "You're not a failure. What makes you think that?"

Sean hesitated. And Colin waited. *Come on, kid. Once—just once—be real with me.*

The mask came on again. "I like my job. And give me back my damn money."

Colin put the credit cards, bank card and miscellaneous bills into his pocket. Then he took out his wallet and extracted two fives. He pushed them across the table to Sean.

"Here's your first week's allowance. If it's not the going rate for allowances, we'll renegotiate."

Sean didn't take the money. He just stalked out of the room.

"SIT," ALEX SAID.

She prodded Colin down in front of the old microfilm machine at the *Silver Lake Herald*. It felt good to take charge of Colin's problems for a change. After their visit to Spokane two days ago, she'd felt dragged down by the enormity of her own. She'd tried to cope by plunging into her work and had given her keyboard a workout expanding her writings on the Type R male. That was when she'd gotten the idea: if she couldn't chase away the ghosts in her life, she could help Colin chase away one of the ghosts in *his*.

"I still don't see how this will help," Colin said.

"Look at it this way. Herbie never gives you an unbiased view of your father, so you have to go to a source that at least *tries* to be unbiased—the press. Sobriety doesn't have its own newspaper. So, for our purposes, we have to refer to the *Silver Lake Herald*."

"Right," Colin said, sounding unconvinced nevertheless.

She sat in a chair beside him and began loading a roll of microfilm into the machine.

"Guess you do this kind of thing a lot," he said.

"Research is my middle name." She *was* always looking for answers, one way or another. She cranked the handle that spooled the film forward. "Okay, this should be right around the time your father was in high school...here we go..."

An hour later, Alex had to admit that the *Silver Lake Herald* made for some pretty monotonous reading. The whole time they worked her gaze kept straying to Colin. And she kept remembering what it had been like to lie in his arms. To make love to him.

Her body heated, even as she sat beside him. What was wrong with her? Didn't she realize what a mistake the lovemaking had been? She'd done nothing but stir up more conflicted feelings. Yearning for Colin to put his arms around her again...fearing that he would. She was in constant tumult now.

Closing her eyes, she willed her emotions to be still. It did no good. When she opened her eyes, she saw that Colin was watching her instead of the screen. "Did you find anything?" she asked.

"Yes." His eyes traveled over her face. And then he placed his hand on her knee.

"Colin..."

"Don't tell me not to think about it. Because you're thinking about it, too."

She glanced away. "It's impossible," she whispered.

"Are you going to run from me again?"

She wished there were more people in the office right now, so she'd have an excuse to avoid this conversation. But she and Colin were alone.

"I unpacked my suitcase, if that's what you mean," she reluctantly said at last. "But, Colin, I never came here to stay. I came to get a job done."

"Are you finished researching me, Alex?"

Now she couldn't help gazing at him. "I think I'm just about done."

Discontent flickered across his face. "Type R male all figured out—that it?"

"Not exactly." She clenched her hands in her lap. She didn't know how to explain it to him: sometimes he made her feel so safe, but other times all she felt was that terrible unease, the one she'd felt when she'd first seen that video of him. She didn't know what it meant. She could understand being afraid of fire. But afraid of Colin? *Why?* The question tortured her, perhaps more than all the others combined.

He studied her another moment with that dissatisfied expression, and then he turned back to the microfilm machine.

"Here's a piece on my dad. Nothing new—just something about basketball."

They kept looking and found a few more articles: an announcement of Thomas's wedding to

Jessie Hamilton, a write-up on how he'd been decorated for bravery. Pilot Thomas McIntyre, the hero. Nothing new, indeed.

"I'm sorry, Colin. I thought maybe we'd find something."

"It was worth a try," he said gruffly.

She respooled the microfilm and slid the roll back into its box. Then she turned off the machine. "Have you talked to anyone else who knew your father?"

"Everybody in Sobriety has stories to tell about him. But that's all they are—stories."

Alex felt that Colin had spent a great deal of his life chasing the illusion of his father, trying to catch up. She wished she knew how to help him.

"Look," she said, "it's noon and we're both hungry. Let's just get out of here."

CHAPTER TWELVE

THE SILVER LAKE CANTINA had tables right at lakeside. Alex and Colin sat shaded by an umbrella as they both ordered the trout and the romaine salad. When the food arrived, everything looked good; Alex just wished her appetite wasn't so fickle these days. One minute she was hungry, the next her stomach was in knots. Right now Colin didn't appear that enthused about lunch, either. He seemed to be eating because there was something in front of him.

"Colin," Alex said, "I've known you only a short while, and already I can tell what a strong person you are inside. But strength has its weaknesses, too. You idolized your father, along with everybody else in this little town. Unlike everybody else, though, you got caught up in using his life as a measuring stick for your own."

She stopped speaking and tried to read Colin's expression. Reading expressions was a habit she'd acquired as a psychologist. You could generally tell when you were driving a point home with a patient, and when your words had shot wide of the mark. With Colin, though, it was impossible to read what he was thinking.

"If your father was as perfect as people say, he'd be a saint and not a man," Alex went on. "Today we tried to find something to make him human. We didn't succeed, but you have to keep trying. You *have* to humanize the legend that was Thomas McIntyre. Perhaps then you can quit trying to prove you're as good as your father—and start living your life for yourself."

He didn't say anything for a minute, just watched the boat drifting in the distance, white sails glinting in the sun. At last he stirred.

"Of course I've considered all this before, Alex—believe me. I've tried to make my dad human. But it hasn't been easy. I keep searching my own memories of him, looking for who he really was." He stopped, then after another long moment he went on.

"I remember one time... I guess I was pretty young, maybe six or seven, and I brought a stray dog home. Neither of my parents was very happy about it. They kept threatening to get rid of it. It was a rotten dog, too—chewed everything it could get its teeth on, barked for hours. I swear my dad hated that animal. One day he came home and found that the dog had destroyed his favorite pair of shoes. I thought that was it, for sure. Except later that night I walked into the living room and saw my dad sitting on the couch, giving that dog a pet behind the ears. The dog was in heaven, and my dad looked at me and said, 'Dumbest dog I ever met. Doesn't take much to make him happy, does it?' Then my dad said we were keeping the dog—because how could you give away anything that dumb.''

"And you did?" Alex asked.

"Sure. We named him Walter, and started hiding our shoes. And then…my dad signed up for another tour in Vietnam.'' Colin gazed at her. "Hey, enough about me. We should be working on your past, not mine.''

She set down her fork. "I tried, didn't I? We did the hypnosis thing, didn't we?''

"You have to go to Montana,'' he said.

It was the last thing she wanted to hear.

But maybe it was the one thing she needed to hear.

THE WILD WEST THEATER was one of Sobriety's landmarks. It had been built in the mining heyday of the 1870s. Maybe it was a bit decrepit now, a bit musty, but it harbored the excitement of long-past stage shows and vaudeville acts. The audience there tonight was good-sized—the summer crowd pouring in.

Herb, Colin and Alex sat in the very front row. Mysteriously, Herb had insisted that he and Colin come. Alex just happened to show up and take the seat next to them. Where the heck was Sean, though?

"Take it easy," Herb said. "Just kick back and see what happens."

Colin glanced at Alex. "Do you know what's going on?"

"Only that Herbie called me about an hour ago and told me to get over here. He wouldn't say why. Have to admit I'm intrigued."

"Take a lesson," Herb said to Colin. "Dr. Alex trusts me."

Against his better judgment, Colin settled back in his seat and tried to relax.

"Tourism's up," Herb said, "thanks to me."

"Let me guess. You're going to start selling tickets for your own act."

Alex glanced over curiously, but Colin wasn't yet ready to tell her his grandfather was the town ghost. Herb had staged a couple of more hauntings, and the last time he'd almost been caught.

Now the heavy red stage curtains were dragging open, then the show began. Colin knew what to expect. For as long as he could remember, Old

West melodrama had been a staple of the theater's summer season. The play would have the coy heroine, the strutting hero, the mustachioed villain. The actors would play the story broadly, for laughs.

Tonight the heroine was acted by none other than Colin's former flame Tina Scott. That was nothing new—Tina often took center stage. The surprise was the actor playing the heroine's kid brother…none other than Colin's own son, TV celebrity Sean McIntyre.

Herb chuckled. "Got you good, didn't I?"

"Why'd you keep it such a secret?"

"The boy thought you'd disapprove."

Colin watched the stage. Sean's role was minor, but he was doing it well, giving his character just the right touch, allowing the other actors to have the spotlight. He was hardly recognizable in a cowboy hat that came down over his ears.

The show was over too quickly. Or so it seemed to Colin. Despite the predictable plot, the barely adequate jokes, the overdone costumes, he had thoroughly enjoyed every moment. Much to his astonishment, his son was a damn good actor.

Afterward, the entire cast got two curtain calls, and several members of the audience crowded backstage.

"You coming?" Herb asked, heading backstage himself.

"In a minute. I'll let people clear out first."

Soon the seats around Colin and Alex were empty. "He's good," Colin said at last. "Damn good. I'll admit that I've never watched his TV show much. But seeing him onstage like that... He's good, that's all."

"And you wished otherwise?" Alex murmured.

"Yeah, I suppose I did. I'd always hoped acting would be just a phase for him. But he has talent. A lot of it. And that means he has to take it seriously." Colin paused. "That means *I* have to take it seriously, too, which I sure as hell don't want to do. I just want my son to have a normal life." Colin stood. "Shall we go congratulate him?"

"Maybe you should go back there on your own," she said.

He thought about it, and then he shook his head. "No. Maybe Sean and I really do need an intermediary. And you're the one he's elected."

She didn't seem thrilled, but she went with him to see his son.

BACKSTAGE, THE FIRST THING Alex noticed was how stunning Tina Scott looked in a bustle skirt, shirtwaist and straw boater. Admirers crowded around her, most of them male. As soon as Tina spied Colin, she peeled away from her suitors. Colin, however, was already headed toward Sean.

Tina sighed with regret. "Isn't that just like him—walking away when you've fallen for him the most?"

"I wouldn't know," Alex said as neutrally as possible.

Tina looked at her consideringly. "Think he won't do it to *you?* The two of you may be an item now, but end of summer's coming soon."

Alex frowned. "Colin and I aren't an *item.*"

"Oh, knock it off," Tina said inelegantly. "By now everybody knows about you two. Of course, I was probably the *first* to figure it out."

"I don't get it. If you're so sure Colin and I have something going, why did you call him the day I was trying to leave?"

Tina shrugged. "Oh, I don't know. Just another of my little tactics," she said cheerfully. "I thought it would make me look noble to Colin— inform him out of the kindness of my heart that his latest paramour is about to fly the coop. Besides, I *do* like a little competition. Keeps things interesting."

"How could I forget. The game's usually too easy...you welcome a challenge."

Tina smiled. "Absolutely. And here's how I see it. If he doesn't dump you first, you'll dump *him.*

You already have one foot out the door." She sailed off to rejoin her admirers.

Alex stood there for a minute, feeling aggravated. She wanted to argue that Tina couldn't possibly know anything about her and Colin. But the phrase "one foot out the door" stuck in her mind.

Colin and Sean stood together a short distance away. From here, Alex could tell their conversation had ground to a halt. If she knew Sean, the conversation hadn't been much to begin with. She went over to them.

"Sean, you did great."

"Yeah?"

He didn't act like some precocious TV star. Instead he seemed genuinely pleased and embarrassed by her compliment. "It was great," she repeated. "How many more performances?"

"Every night the next two weeks. Matinee Saturday and Sunday. If I'm not *grounded*," he added with elaborate sarcasm.

"You're not," Colin replied with elaborate patience.

It occurred to Alex that maybe she should join Herbie and let the two younger-generation McIntyre males take another stab at communicating. But this time, they both gave her a look that implored, *Hey, please don't go.*

So she stuck around. But that phrase kept echoing in her mind: *one foot out the door...*

STEVE'S OUTFITTERS, where Alex had bought all her backpacking gear, occupied one of the narrow brick buildings on Sobriety's Main Street. It was full to overflowing with camping supplies: tents, cookstoves, collapsible chairs, rain ponchos, inflatable mats. The place was so crowded with paraphernalia that Alex and Colin had to squeeze down the aisles. She wondered why Colin had brought her here today. He had that intense look again of a man who'd come up with a plan.

"Okay, spill it," she said. "I hardly think we're here to buy me more hiking gear."

"You already bought out the store, so we can't do that." He paused. "Maybe I'll buy out the store, instead."

She examined a blouse in khaki. "Hmm... considering another trip into the mountains?"

"I'm serious," he said. "I've just about decided to buy this place outright from Steve."

Alex stared at him with full attention now. "You're joking."

"He's been thinking about selling. And I've been thinking about changing my life."

"So you want to be a...store owner."

"Perhaps." He glanced around reflectively. "Of course, I'd give the place a major overhaul. Less clutter, more variety. You'd be able to get your biking supplies here, too. And why not canoes, as long as I'm at it?"

"Colin, you're doing it again—acting like you can just...settle down. But I keep telling you— you're a rescuer. You need excitement. It's kind of the way Tina Scott needs a challenge when it comes to men. If the chase is too predictable, she gets bored—"

"What does Tina Scott have to do with it?" Colin looked disgruntled.

"She's just an example. I'm trying to make a point here. And the point is...you can't stop being who you are."

He paced farther along the aisle, sidestepping a rack of mosquito repellent. "Alex, something's got to change in my life. I need to give Sean something different from what he has in California. A place where he can just kick back and be a kid. Idaho could be it. Okay, maybe my plan hasn't worked so well this far, but if I lived here permanently...he could spend more and more time with me. I know Beth would be willing to work it out. She's reasonable when it comes to Sean. We both want what's best for him."

"You've told me that before," Alex murmured.

"But you can't give him what he needs unless you think about what's best for *you.*"

He turned, and she saw discontent in his expression.

"I've just about decided to quit my job in California. Besides, maybe Sean needs a more… normal father."

"Like a store owner."

"You make it sound like I want to be a mortician."

Alex shook her head. "I don't have the answers for you, Colin. I just know you're not meant for the backwater."

"Thought you were starting to like Idaho," he said.

Now she picked up a miniature flashlight and tried it out. "I have no complaints about Sobriety or Silver Lake. For somebody like me, here would probably be perfect. Peaceful, laid-back. Plenty of sunshine and water. Very appealing, I have to admit."

"Glad to hear it," he remarked. "Because I was thinking I might ask you to stay here with me."

The flashlight went flying out of her hand. She bent down, grabbed it again, then fiddled with it. By the time she'd discovered that it still worked, she had a little of her composure back. She stood up and faced Colin.

"I guess I didn't quite understand."

"I was clear," he grumbled. "I'm thinking of asking you to stay with me."

"As in…live at your house on the lake."

"That's the idea," he said. "And I suppose marriage is an option."

She gave a strangled laugh. "Colin, is this a *proposal?*"

He looked more dissatisfied than ever. "Could be. But I never understood all that business about a man proposing, a woman accepting. When the time's right, the two people involved should have a joint discussion…make the appropriate decision."

"And we're having that discussion *now?*"

"Hell, no. I'm just trying to point out how things could go in the future."

She lost her composure once more. Swiveling, she went in the opposite direction, fighting through racks of down parkas and fleece.

"Running away from me again, Alex?"

She stopped, looking around a bit desperately. Across from her was another rack of backpacking blouses. She grabbed one at random. "I just want to try this on." With that, she disappeared into the small dressing room.

She stared at herself in the mirror. Her cheeks were flushed, her eyes darker than usual: the classic physical manifestations of distress, confusion...longing.

The thought of living with Colin, sharing the day-to-day details of existence, and at night... every night...sharing something else, too, was enough to take her breath away.

With a moan, she pressed her hands to her cheeks. That was a fantasy, nothing more. It couldn't possibly happen. Too many obstacles stood in the way. And always that disturbing fact hung at the edge of her consciousness: something about Colin frightened her. She didn't know what it was, but it never quite left her. Always it haunted her.

Trying to buy time, she took a while to unbutton her shirt. She took some more time buttoning up the new blouse. And then she went out to Colin.

He surveyed her. "It's okay, but the color's a little off." He pulled another blouse from the rack. "Here, try this."

"I don't think either of us is really concerned about the status of my wardrobe right now." She folded her arms and confronted him. "Okay, here's how I see it. You've formed some kind of vague picture in your mind of the life you *should* offer your son. It includes a 'normal' profession, perhaps even a steady partner. You picture me as the partner, and I suppose I don't look so bad to you."

''Now you make it sound like I'm proposing a business merger. I think you know by now that I see a relationship with you as anything but.''

''Colin, you're trying to fit me into your scenario, but *you* don't even belong in it, let alone me.''

He hung the blouse back on the rack. ''I take it that's a no.''

Regret stirred deep inside her. At this moment, she would have given anything to say yes.

''It's a no,'' she confirmed, her voice soft. ''I've already made a plan of my own. I'm leaving Idaho for real this time. Except I'm not headed back to Chicago right away. I'm…going to Montana.'' There. She'd said the words she'd been dreading. And they finally made her decision real and concrete.

Colin didn't say anything at first. From his expression, she couldn't tell what he was thinking. But at last he spoke.

''Of course you're going to Montana. And I'm going with you.''

''Why on earth—''

''You've already said no once. Don't say it again. You're going to Montana to face something that has you waking up at night crying and in a sweat. And you're damn well not going alone.''

EARLY NEXT MORNING, Alex and Colin were on the road. Their first stop would be Missoula, Montana, well across the state line. From there they'd head to Butte, and Bozeman, and Billings, then, finally, on to Penrose…Alex's hometown.

As the Jeep traveled along the highway, Alex felt like a heavy weight was lodged inside her. She wanted to tell Colin to slow down—anything to delay the end of their journey. She didn't want to go home, especially to a place that had never *seemed* like home.

"I still wonder if I'm doing the right thing," she said.

"You're doing the right thing."

"Thanks for coming with me," she said after another moment. "It's above and beyond the call of duty."

He smiled wryly. "It's always a good idea to take a trip with somebody who's just turned down your proposal of marriage."

She glanced at him sharply. "I thought you didn't believe in marriage proposals."

"Okay, it was a proposal to consider a *discussion* of marriage at some point in the future."

"Colin…you weren't really serious, were you?"

"Kind of think I was, Alex."

She huddled on her side of the Jeep, the regret threatening to engulf her now.

"Try settling down," she said. "Just try it. I'm willing to bet that in less than a month you'll be going stir-crazy."

"I'll be taking you up on that bet. Because yesterday I called my boss in California and told him I was quitting my job."

She gazed at him in dismay. "Oh, no. You can't do that. You're—you're a *rescuer.*"

"Afraid you're going to lose your guinea pig, Alex?"

That wasn't it at all. Her research of Colin had taken directions she could never possibly have imagined. And by now the two of them had gone beyond research…way beyond.

"Your boss probably wasn't too happy with your decision," she said. "Even if he does think you're too reckless."

"He tried to talk me out of it. But my mind's made up."

"And you're really going to buy that store?" she asked.

"If Steve really wants to sell."

He was making a big mistake, but Alex didn't know how to convince him.

And meanwhile, every mile brought her closer and closer to Montana. Closer and closer to her nightmare.

CHAPTER THIRTEEN

COLIN WASN'T IMPRESSED with Penrose. It was a drab little town, with nothing to distinguish it from a hundred other drab little towns off the main track. But maybe he was already prejudiced against the place because of Alex. Something bad had happened to her here...and he didn't like bad things happening to Alex.

Her mother lived on a nondescript side street where the houses were made of cinder block. It was near dusk when Colin pulled to a stop in front of Gayle Robbins's home. The trip had been long, made longer still by frequent stops. Colin had sensed that Alex was in no hurry to get here, so he'd followed as many diversions along the way as possible.

She swung open the passenger door. "You don't have to come with me," she said, her voice tight. "You can meet her later."

He went with her up the path to the door. He already knew Alex hadn't told her mother she was coming. Now she stood, head bowed, as if she'd suddenly run out of steam. Colin was the one who pressed the buzzer.

A few moments later, the porch light came on and the door opened to reveal a blond woman in her mid-fifties or so. She stared at the two of them.

"Alex," she said at last, her tone curiously flat.

"Hello, Mom."

Most people would be glad to see their children. Not Gayle Robbins, apparently. She just stood on the other side of the screen door, as though hoping Alex would vanish.

"Mom...I know you're surprised to see me—but don't worry. We won't be imposing. We'll be staying at a hotel. This is Colin McIntyre, by the way. Colin...my mother."

She'd said this in a rush. Colin wondered how it would feel if you had to apologize to a parent for your presence.

Gayle Robbins started. "Of course. I'm forgetting myself. Please...come in."

A short time later, both Colin and Alex were seated in the living room. The decor was unexpectedly eclectic: an Indian print couch, framed Mexican tiles on the walls, modern copper and tin sculptures everywhere. Colin examined the sculpture on the coffee table—a free-form woman whirling in a solitary dance.

"Is this your new work?" Alex asked her mother.

"Yes. Just some experimenting."

"It's very good. Maybe the best you've done yet."

"Thank you, dear."

Despite the endearment, Gayle Robbins sounded formal. She looked formal, as well, her clothes too coordinated, too polished.

She was playing the part of hostess, bringing out wine and sherry, asking if they were hungry. They took the drinks, declined the food. Gayle sat down across from them.

"Well, how did you two meet?" she asked.

"Mom—" Alex burst out, "stop acting as if you're trying to be polite to unwelcome guests."

"You're not unwelcome, Alex," Gayle said carefully, "but this *is* unexpected. In the past, you've made it clear how much you dislike coming back here."

"It's not you. It's…the town. It's everything…" Alex stood abruptly. "You know what? I really am tired. It's been a long day. Colin and I are going to go find a hotel. We'll come back tomorrow. And then we'll talk."

"I have to work tomorrow," Gayle said. "I wish I'd had more notice—I could have taken some time off to entertain you."

Alex clenched her hands. "We're not here to be entertained... I think you already know that. Look, I'll come back tomorrow afternoon, after you're home. And then—I'll just see you then."

Gayle made an effort to say how much she'd enjoyed meeting Colin, et cetera, et cetera, but Alex was already out the door. By the time Colin climbed into the Jeep, she was in the passenger seat, staring straight ahead.

"You might as well say it," she told him. "I'm a coward. I should have confronted her right away."

"I'm not saying anything. You'll do this in your own time."

"You've been saying that all day! It's so damn annoying..." She buried her head in her hands. "Oh, look, Colin, I'm not angry at you. I'm angry at myself. I bolted from that house first chance I got. Everything just seemed to be closing in, but that's no excuse to be a coward."

He managed to bring her into a hug, made awkward by the gearshift knob between them. "Give yourself a break, Alex."

"I don't know if I can, not while I'm in this town. Can we just go find a hotel?"

There was one about a mile away—clean, colorless. Pretty much like the rest of the town. When they went to register, Alex asked firmly for two rooms. Colin didn't object, but it was too bad. They ended up in adjoining suites that were on special rate. Alex told Colin she wanted to go to sleep right away, but he knew she had to be hungry—they hadn't eaten since about three. He ordered room service: steak and baked potatoes. Unoriginal, perhaps, but the meal got the job done. After they'd eaten, Alex said good-night and closed the door between them.

Colin sat in his room, feeling a curious sense of letdown. He didn't know what he'd expected. At the very least, he'd hoped his presence would make this visit easier for Alex. Instead she was shutting him out.

He didn't have a lot of hope for tomorrow.

"THIS IS THE SCHOOL I went to. Mrs. Baxter was my favorite teacher. Third grade. Back then, I wanted to be a veterinarian when I grew up—go figure."

Alex was taking Colin on the Penrose tour. He couldn't say that he was enjoying it. So far they'd seen the new mall, the equally new multiplex theater, the bowling alley-skating rink and the Penrose House, where you could admire the belongings of the town founder. But Colin didn't want to be around Alex the tour guide. He wanted to be around Alex the woman. He wanted, especially, for her to need him. Today, however, she'd been making a special effort to show him how independent and self-contained she was.

This school, at least, had something to do with Alex herself. The two of them migrated to the playground, where they sat in swings which were too small. Except for a few kids hanging upside down on the jungle gym, the yard was deserted. It was summer vacation.

"I used to love going to school," Alex said. "It was a way to get out of the house, where everything was so *quiet*. Here there was noise, and I could be with my friends. I was one of those disgustingly attentive students. You know, the little girl who sits in the front row and always raises her hand."

"Your teachers probably didn't complain too much."

"I rebelled in junior high," she said, as if to redeem herself. "I went through a very irresponsible phase. Then I reformed just enough in high school to get a college scholarship."

"I was always a lousy student," Colin said. "I'm lucky I got to college at all, or that the air force ended up taking me. But you really don't want to sit here trading school stories, Alex. You want to find out why you left this town as soon as you graduated and why you hate coming back."

She pushed her toes into the dirt to get the swing going. "I'll see my mother later on. I don't know what else I can do."

"Same thing we did in Silver Lake. We go to the local library and try to get some information from that unbiased source of yours...the press."

Now she held very still, her hands wrapped around the chains of the swing. "What do you mean, Colin?"

"Think about it. We're fairly certain that you were in some type of fire as a child, and that it happened in this town. There are always records of fires."

She looked scared. "You're right," she said, almost bleakly. "We might be able to find something."

"It's worth a try."

She hesitated. He wasn't going to press her if she decided to say no. He'd meant what he said about letting her do this in her own time. But finally she nodded reluctantly.

"Let's go."

UNLIKE THE PUBLIC LIBRARY in Silver Lake, Idaho, the Penrose Public Library was housed in a brand-new building, with an adjacent garden kept up by the local rose club. From where Alex sat with Colin in the reading room, she could look out the window at the rosebushes, many of them in full bloom. Everything was much nicer here than in the cramped library where she'd spent so many of her girlhood hours, whiling away the time with story-books or doing research for school reports. Even back then she'd loved research…finding patterns, searching for answers.

She and Colin were looking for answers right now, old newspapers spread out on the table be-tween them. Despite the revamped physical sur-roundings, no one had bothered to copy the news-papers onto microfilm. She and Colin were examining the real thing.

They'd started at the very beginning—the year of Alex's birth. That was her idea. When you were dealing with repressed memories, you had to con-sider that they could go quite far back. Since she and Colin had embarked on this, they might as well be thorough about it.

The only problem was, it made for slow going. They had to scrutinize every edition, making sure they didn't miss anything. By the time they'd reached the year of Alex's second birthday, they had fifteen minutes left till closing. So far they'd read an article about a restaurant fire over on Jer-emy Street, and brief items on two house fires. None of the details in the three cases fit Alex's

THE RESCUER

snatches of memory. Certainly none of the names were familiar.

She glanced at her watch. "Time to quit."

"We can always come back tomorrow. And we could head down to the police station, check their records, too."

The sense of foreboding she'd had all day only intensified. "It was my idea to be thorough, but still…"

Colin stretched. "It's just an idea."

"I wish you wouldn't pretend not to be pushing me, when that's what you're doing." She'd spoken more sharply than she'd intended. "I'm sorry," she said. She seemed to be apologizing to Colin a lot this trip.

"Okay," he said, "maybe I am pushing you. I want you to get this damned thing out in the open so you can get on with your life."

"Colin, you can't really want me to stay in Idaho with you and live in that house and—"

"I love you, Alex."

He said the words so offhandedly that at first she didn't think she'd heard right. She looked around the library, as if one of the other patrons could clarify the matter for her.

Her gaze came back to Colin. He was observing her steadily, with a slight frown.

"Guess I didn't really have it figured out until

now," he said. "The part about being in love with you, anyway. But it's the truth, and I can't see what's wrong with it."

Her heart was pounding, and she had to stand up. "You know something, Colin? It just so happens that maybe I'm in love with you, too. Maybe I didn't figure it out until just now, either, but I don't see how it does you or me a whole lot of good. Because I *can't* go on with my life until I find out what happened to me all those years ago...and what's in store for me. And *your* life's pretty much a mess, too!"

With that, she walked out of the library.

THAT EVENING, WHEN ALEX showed up at her mother's house, Gayle hadn't yet returned from work. Alex hunkered down on the porch steps to wait for her. How many times had she sat on this porch as a young girl, dreaming of the day she'd be able to leave Montana and make her own life. She'd managed to do both. But now, being back...she wondered if she'd truly escaped after all.

Remembering what she'd told Colin in the library didn't help. Practically admitting that she loved him... Had she merely been swept up in the moment?

How could you love someone and be afraid of him at the same time?

This was another question she couldn't escape.

Just then her mother's car pulled into the driveway. Gayle climbed out and came toward Alex.

"Hello," she said.

Alex got to her feet. "Hi."

"Where's your friend Colin?"

"I told him that you and I should...have some time alone."

Gayle concentrated on unlocking the front door. "He seems very nice."

Alex didn't answer, because she sensed more was coming. She wasn't disappointed.

"So soon after your divorce, though. I assume the divorce *is* final...."

Alex followed her mother into the house. "Yes, it is. But Colin and I aren't a couple." She stopped, wondering why she was explaining herself to her mother.

"I'm famished," Gayle said. "Have you eaten?"

"No. I'm not particularly hungry, though."

"Nonsense. I'll fix something for both of us." Gayle seemed glad to have a project. "Make yourself comfortable, Alex. Look around—see if you like some of the changes in the place." Then she went into the kitchen, leaving Alex to stand alone in the middle of the living room.

Alex couldn't remain still for long. She went across the hall and opened the door to her old bedroom. Signs of her existence here had vanished; it had become a workroom, with bits of colored glass, strips of metal and bags of beads scattered on the desk. Alex even saw a soldering gun. She closed the door and went back to the living room, but she couldn't bring herself to sit down.

Gayle served tomato soup, and pumpernickel that she'd toasted. Alex recalled those toasted slices of pumpernickel from her childhood. She still disliked the taste of them, and she set down a piece after only one bite. The soup she barely sampled.

"Why aren't there ever any pictures of Dad?" she asked suddenly.

Gayle took small, measured spoonfuls of soup. "What do you mean?"

"As far back as I can remember, there've never been any pictures of him around."

"His death was very painful for me." Gayle spoke without emotion. "I put his photographs away right afterward, and somehow I just didn't bring them out again. It never bothered you before, Alex."

"It bothered me. I remember asking you about

it…but you never wanted to talk about him. Why?''

Gayle skimmed the soup with her spoon, making an effort to carry on the conversation normally. ''When people die, it's difficult to talk about them.''

''Not everybody feels that way.'' Alex thought about Herb, surrounded by his family photographs, unable to stop talking about his dead son. Maybe that was the better way.

''Talking about memories can cheapen them.''

Gayle sounded as if she were repeating carefully rehearsed words. Alex crumpled her napkin, so keyed up she could scarcely speak.

''What happened to me when I was a child? Why won't you tell me?''

At last Gayle set down her spoon. She slid her bowl to one side. ''I don't understand, Alex. First you call me and berate me on the phone, and now…''

''I just need to know.'' Alex felt as though someone was compressing her chest and she had to fight to breathe. ''There was a fire, wasn't there? And someone there with me. Someone threatening me somehow…I was so scared. I couldn't move…''

''Stop.'' The word burst from Gayle, and her

face had gone white. "Stop, Alex. You don't know what you're talking about."

"Then tell me! What happened?"

Gayle's entire body tensed. "There's nothing for you to know. I have always protected you."

Alex pushed back her chair. When she stood, she was trembling so much she had to grip the edge of the table. "Is that what you're doing now—protecting me? It's not working, Mom. It won't stop the nightmare. It comes almost every night now. I try not going to sleep. I try everything…but nothing works. Whatever happened is haunting me. Don't you see? It won't let me alone."

Gayle stood, too, confronting Alex from the other side of the table. Her eyes looked hard, even with the unshed tears welling in them.

"I have protected you," she repeated. "It was the one thing I hoped I could do for you. It wasn't a mistake. I won't *let* it be a mistake. Not after all these years. Do you understand, Alex?"

COLIN SMOOTHED BACK the hair from Alex's face. They lay on her bed at the hotel. The door between their rooms was open now, and he intended for it to remain that way. Enough of her trying to carry the burden alone.

"I guess things went pretty badly with your mother," he said.

She closed her eyes briefly. "Awful. She made me feel so damn guilty for even asking about the past. And she wouldn't answer, Colin—she just wouldn't. I tell you, she's like a wall. You keep pounding and pounding your fists on it...but there's no give."

He smoothed away another strand from her face. "So we'll go back to the library. And wherever else we have to to get the answers."

She gazed at him, her eyes haunted. "I'm afraid of the answers, Colin."

"I know." He kissed her, and it was a few seconds before he felt her response. "Want me to leave?" he murmured.

"No...don't go." She put her arms around him, suddenly fierce. "I know it's wrong to want this now..."

"It's not wrong. It's what you need...what both of us need."

She didn't deny it. This time she was the one who kissed him, almost frantically. She held him close and made clear what she wanted next.

Their coming together wasn't leisurely, like the first time they'd made love. They were both in a hurry now, as if they'd denied themselves too long. Their clothes were removed awkwardly, in a rush.

Then, almost immediately, Alex wrapped her legs around him, asking for all he could offer. And yet he sensed her distance. Their bodies touched, gave each other pleasure, but he couldn't reach her heart or her mind. She closed her eyes, as if to keep him from the most secret part of her. They moved together…release came. But all along there was an emptiness.

Alex rolled away and pulled the sheet over her. Although she didn't say anything, he knew she wanted him to leave. Again he smoothed her hair.

"It's okay," he told her.

"No—it's not. If that's making love…"

"It doesn't always have to be perfect."

"Do you really believe that?"

"Yes, I do," he said. "Two people stay together long enough they'll have ups and downs."

"We're not going to stay together." Her voice was hollow.

"Don't be too sure of anything right now." He wondered what he could say to get through to her. So far, he wasn't doing a very good job. "I meant what I said, Alex. About loving you."

"It doesn't make any difference."

"Hell, Alex—it's not like you to be apathetic."

She sat up, holding the sheet to her. "You're angry." She almost sounded glad—as though she wanted a fight.

"I'm not angry."

"Don't deny it. Jonathan did that. At first he'd tell me he wasn't mad. Then he'd get quiet. And then…he'd let the anger build, and it would end up coming out after all. In a very ugly way."

"I'm not your ex."

"Just say it, then. Just say you're ticked."

She really was spoiling for a fight. Maybe it was her way of pushing him away.

"I'm not ticked," he said. "And if you want an argument, Alex…you're not going to get one. Not from me, anyway."

She sank back against the pillows. "I'm sorry, Colin."

"Maybe you need to yell at somebody."

"Oh, great," she said. "Use you for sex and then yell at you. Quite a relationship we have going here."

"It's a start," he said. He kissed her one last time, and then he went across to his own room.

But he left the door open between them.

CHAPTER FOURTEEN

THE SOBS WOKE HIM UP, sometime in the middle of the night. Instantly he was out of bed, crossing to Alex's room. A few seconds later, he'd gathered her into his arms. She clung to him, crying.

"Damn," he said, holding her against him. He'd never wanted to protect any woman the way he wanted to protect Alex. But he'd also never known any woman so determined to refuse his help. Already she was pulling away, as if she regretted this momentary lapse.

"Want to tell me about it?" he asked.

"Not particularly."

He turned on the bedside lamp. Alex grimaced as the light fell over her. She wore a pair of light blue cotton pajamas, and they made her look more vulnerable than ever. As if sensing his thoughts, she grabbed a tissue and blotted the tears from her cheeks.

"Crying in your sleep," she muttered. "Ridiculous."

If she thought he was going to leave, she could

forget it. He settled on the edge of the bed. Alex glanced at him uneasily. Okay, so he was naked— he wasn't a big believer in pajamas himself. But they'd already made love…it seemed they could be comfortable around each other.

Then again, maybe not. Alex just sat there with her knees drawn up, and now she was making an effort not to look at him. Grumbling, he went to his own room. When he returned, he was wearing his jeans.

"Better?" he asked as he sat back down on the bed.

She didn't say anything at first. Then at last she took a deep, unsteady breath. "The nightmare was different this time. But so many of the feelings were the same—me feeling helpless…feeling small. And someone looming over me. Someone…hurting me."

Colin listened intently. "Hurting you how, Alex?"

She pressed her hands against her temples. "I think—I think he's taking hold of my arm. And…shaking me. And he knows he's hurting me. He *knows*…"

"Who is it?" Colin asked, very quietly.

Again she didn't answer. She lowered her forehead against her knees. A moment later, when she lifted her face, she wore an oddly calm expression.

"I have to go see my mother," she said. "And I have to do it right now."

ALEX ZIPPED UP HER FLEECE jacket as she slid out the passenger side of the Jeep.

"Sure you don't want me to go with you?"

Colin sounded concerned. She was grateful to him for coming on this trip with her, for offering support when she didn't know how to give him anything in return. But this was something she had to do alone.

"I'll be fine," she said.

"I'll be right here."

In the darkness, she went up the walk to her mother's house. She rang the buzzer twice—hard. And then she rang it again.

After what seemed a long time, the porch light came on, and a few seconds later the door swung open. Her mother stood there, clutching her robe against her body.

"Alex, it's the middle of the night. What on earth is wrong—are you all right?"

"I need to talk to you, Mom." Without waiting for an invitation, Alex stepped inside the house. She turned and confronted her mother. "I have to ask you again. Why aren't there any photographs of my father?"

"Alex, I can't believe you came here to talk about *photographs*—"

"Actually I didn't." Alex listened to the brittle sound of her own voice. "I came here to ask you if my father was ever abusive to me. I suspect he was. I suspect he wasn't the greatest guy in the world, and that's why you can't even bear to have a picture of him around."

Gayle had gone very white. She went into the living room and sank into a chair. Then she bent her head, as if to shield herself. But Alex wouldn't let her hide—not anymore.

"Tell me, Mom. You have to tell me. Because the nightmare won't stop coming."

Gayle lifted her head. A look almost of fury contorted her face—but it was a look of despair, too. "You really want to know? Yes, he was abusive, Alex. He threatened me. He hit me. Time and time again. I despised myself for staying with him, but I was so afraid. So very afraid. And then he started doing the same thing to you…" She struggled to her feet. "Are you glad that I told you? Does it help? Does it make things any better?"

Alex stood there, holding her arms against her chest. "No," she whispered. "No, it doesn't make anything better…"

"Leave it alone, Alex. Don't ask me anything else." Gayle's voice was raw. "He's gone. Isn't that enough? The bastard's gone, and you and I are safe. Safe at last…''

Suddenly Alex didn't want to hear any more. She turned and walked out of the house, a peculiar calm surrounding her, as if she were trapped in the eye of a storm. She reached the Jeep and climbed back inside.

''We're leaving town,'' she said to Colin, almost conversationally. ''We're leaving right away.''

Even in the darkness, she could feel him studying her. She didn't flinch from his scrutiny. She merely waited for his questions…all the questions she would push aside.

But he didn't ask any at all. He just started the engine and pulled away from the curb.

KELLY'S SALOON WAS ONE of Sobriety's premiere tourist attractions. Not that that was saying much. Still, the place had lots of Old West atmosphere: a mural of painted ladies over the bar, cocktail waitresses in cowboy hats, live fiddle music every Friday and Saturday night.

Colin sat at the bar and ordered a beer. You had to be grateful for the small things in life, he told himself, such as the fact that it wasn't either Friday or Saturday…and therefore no fiddle music he had to endure.

He didn't want any company, but after a while a man halfway down the bar moved closer to him.

"You're Thomas's boy, aren't you?"

He'd heard that question often enough in his life. "Yes."

"Frank Rowland." The man held out his hand, and Colin shook it. "I used to know your dad pretty well."

Now would come one of the stories about how Thomas McIntyre had been better and brighter than anyone else around.

"Good old Tommy."

Colin found himself starting to pay attention. He'd never heard anyone call his father "Tommy." He gave Frank Rowland a closer look. The guy was probably about sixty, a little on the paunchy side, his hair sparse. He raised his beer in a mock salute.

"Here's to your dad."

Colin drank to that.

"Look, I guess you were just a kid when he died. But I was drinking buddies with Tommy for a while there. Before he went to 'Nam that second time."

Colin ate a pretzel and passed the bowl to Frank.

"You'd never know it to look at me now," said Frank, "but I used to be kind of a scrawny guy— the butt of more than my share of jokes. That's

how I met your dad. I'm in an alley down on Fifth
Street, getting more than my share of jokes from
a couple of real jokers. Things get a little rough,
and before I know it, one of the jokers is using my
face for a punching bag. And then, amazingly, the
second joker steps in and tries to stop it. Only,
stopping it isn't what the first joker has in mind.
So the two start going at it. Your dad was the second joker—the one who won out. He apologized
to me later by buying me a beer. Like I said, we
were drinking buddies for a long while after that.''

Now Frank Rowland gave Colin a sympathetic
look. ''Damn shame the night Tommy died. Damn
shame.''

Colin shook his head. He motioned to the bar-
tender and ordered another round for the both of
them.

''Tell me some more, Frank…tell me more
about my dad.''

ALEX WAS WALKING DOWN Main Street when she
noticed Sean McIntyre looking out the window of
the mining museum. Sean started to wave, then
stopped himself, as if recollecting that any display
of enthusiasm wasn't cool. Alex, however, stepped
inside the museum.

''Hi, Sean. What's up?''

"Nothing." He was still making an effort to be cool.

A middle-aged woman emerged from a room in back. "Sean, I found those labels…oh, hello." She smiled at Alex. "I'm Lillian Prescott. And, no question—you're Dr. Robbins."

"Alex, please."

"Alex it is, then. Sean's helping me organize some of our collections. He's very good at it— although he doesn't like to hear it. I've told him that if he ever wants to leave the entertainment business, he can become a museum curator any day."

Sean got that long-suffering expression common to teenagers who've just been praised by their elders. He took the stack of labels from Lillian, gave Alex an awkward glance and disappeared into the back room. Lillian watched him go.

"He's a good kid, even if he does worry his father and his great-grandpa," she murmured. Then she turned back to Alex. "Guess you know about me," she said matter-of-factly.

Alex wasn't quite certain what she was supposed to know. "Actually…"

"Oh, come on, Herbie's spilled the beans by now, I suppose."

"Afraid not," Alex said apologetically. "I've never heard him mention you."

Lillian raised her eyebrows a bit. "Well, I didn't expect him to be that circumspect. I swore him to secrecy, but still...*you* might as well know. I've been dating Herbie for almost a year now. On the sly, of course."

So, Herbie had a girlfriend.

"Why the secret?" Alex asked.

Lillian sighed. But then she said, "How would you like a cup of coffee?"

It sounded good to Alex. That was how she and Lillian Prescott ended up at Maggie's Diner only a short time later. The afternoon lull meant there were only a few other patrons, and Alex led Lillian to "her" booth in the corner, where privacy was guaranteed. Nonetheless, Lillian spoke in a hushed voice as she stirred sugar into her coffee.

"I suppose you've never heard the rumors about me, either."

Alex couldn't say she had.

"Well, maybe the residents of Sobriety aren't such gossips after all." Lillian almost sounded disappointed. "Everybody thinks that when I visit Boise I'm going to visit a married man."

"And are you?" Alex asked. She felt strangely comfortable with this woman, as if already they'd known each other a long while.

Lillian sighed again. "Once, a long time ago... yes, I did have an affair with an *almost* married man in Boise. He was engaged and suffering from cold feet. I was very, very young and not altogether wise. I finally realized how hopeless and tawdry the situation was, and I came back to Sobriety for good. You may wonder why I've let the rumors continue all these years. Well, at first I thought they made me seem *interesting*—a woman who didn't always live by the rules. And after a while the rumors just stuck, and I didn't bother trying to do anything about them. I just kept on going to Boise for shopping excursions, and I let everybody think what they wanted.''

Alex stirred the tea she'd ordered as usual; today it was lemon verbena. ''You and Herbie being a secret…is that interesting, too?''

Lillian smiled ruefully. ''Serves me right for confessing to a psychologist. The truth is, Alex, at my age you realize you'd better not let your chance for excitement slip by. Seeing Herbie on the sly *does* add that spice of excitement…we're always on the verge of being caught.''

Alex sipped her tea. ''A little excitement never hurt anybody.''

''Seems to me you're being secretive, too—you and Colin. Neither one of you will come right out and make your relationship official. I take it back—the citizens of Sobriety *are* tremendous gossips.''

"I like them anyway," Alex said. "I'll miss them when I leave."

"So, you *are* leaving. That rumor's true, at least."

"Tomorrow or the next day. I'm just wrapping up some loose ends." She wasn't being entirely honest. She'd already wrapped up the loose ends, completed all her research notes on Colin. Right now she was lingering...hanging in limbo. Since returning from Montana two days ago, she'd felt lost. That visit to her mother had only made the shadows in her life worse—the nightmare more frightening. Maybe she should just get back to Chicago as soon as she could. Or maybe she should give in to her longings. Stay here and run to Colin's arms.

"It's not a secret," Alex said. "Colin's said he loves me." The words slipped out so naturally, so easily. Lillian really did seem like the kind of person you could talk to without fear of repercussions. So unlike Alex's mother...

"What's the problem, then?" Lillian asked, refilling her cup from the coffeepot Denise had left on the table.

"Sometimes being in love just isn't enough."

"I don't know if I agree," Lillian said. "The rumor of that so-called affair of mine made for very poor company over the years. Now that Herbie and I are stepping out, I realize how lonely I used to be. This is much better. Even if the old codger *does* drive me nuts sometimes with his silly ideas.''

Maybe Alex would end up having to choose loneliness. Too much stood between her and Colin—way too much. She'd just learned that her father had been a less-than-decent human being. An abusive man. And her husband had bordered on abusive. In fact, the last time she'd seen him he'd crossed that line. Why had she chosen a man apparently so much like her own father? The very idea made her feel sick.

She knew with all her heart that Colin would never hurt anyone. He wasn't like her father or her ex-husband. So why did that murky fear still grip her when she thought of Colin? *Why?*

There were other things, however. Confused images that came to her more and more in her nightmare. That looming presence…her father, no doubt, even though he remained nameless and faceless. Shaking her and hurting her. And then… Dying. Crumpling to the ground before her eyes. Going violently. Not peacefully, in a hospital bed, as her mother had always told her. No. Dying as the flames rose behind him—

''Alex, what's wrong?'' Lillian said, leaning across the table toward her, gazing at her with an expression of concern. "You look as if you're about to faint."

Her heart was pounding, her palms damp. With an effort, she brought herself back to her surroundings: homey Maggie's Diner, where it seemed nothing terrible could ever happen.

But something terrible had happened long ago in Montana. And Alex had the growing conviction that there was another figure in her nightmare. Her mother.

That was the part that scared Alex most of all. Maybe, when you had a husband who beat you and who'd started hurting your daughter, too...maybe you would do anything to be rid of him.

And maybe you would do anything to hide the truth.

TONIGHT WAS HERB'S TURN to cook dinner. Colin was glad—his own attempts at the culinary arts were generally less than successful.

Herb did his usual good job with the food; then Colin and Sean took over as cleanup crew. It didn't exactly make for family togetherness. By now Sean had perfected his ability to reply in surly monosyllables, but as soon as he could, he slouched off to the living room to turn on the television. At least he was watching TV, not *on* it.

Herb came into the kitchen and opened the freezer.

"Still hungry?" Colin asked.

Herb took out the ice cream he'd served at dinner. "Might as well finish this stuff off." He sat down at the table and started spooning some into a bowl. Colin sat down across from him.

"I've been waiting for a good time to say this. But maybe there is no good time. So—here goes. Why didn't you ever tell me that my father was an alcoholic?"

The ice-cream scoop froze halfway to Herb's bowl. "Where the hell did you hear that?"

"Frank Rowland."

"Frank's a drunk himself."

"I don't think so," Colin said.

Herb set down the scoop, not even noticing the ice cream dripping onto the tablecloth. "Your father knew how to handle himself in any situation. Why are you trashing his memory?"

Sean appeared, hovering in the doorway. "What's going on?"

"Nothing," Herb said, his face mottled with anger.

Colin suddenly felt weary. Give him some concrete hardship to fight against, and he could do it. All his life he'd had physical endurance. He knew how to push his muscles, how to make his body go farther and faster. But this emotional stuff…he wasn't so good at that.

"Sean, this is between your great-grandfather and me."

"That sucks," Sean said. "You always say you want to be open about everything. So why the hell do I have to leave?"

"Your language, son. Watch your language."

"Leave the boy be," Herb said. "Let him hear. Your father *was* better." Herb thumped his fist down on the table. "Better than the rest of us. Braver…going back to Vietnam when he'd already put in his time. You think somebody ordinary did that?"

"I don't know, Herb. I don't know why he went back."

"Courage, that's why. Don't you *ever* call him a drunk again."

Colin had nothing more to say. He walked out of the kitchen, went to the living room and just stood there, not knowing what he was going to do next.

Sean followed. "It's no fun, is it?" he said.

Colin looked at his son. "What's no fun?"

"Being the bad guy. Having everybody think they know better than you and telling you what you're doing wrong."

Colin placed a hand on Sean's shoulder. "No, son, it's no fun at all."

CHAPTER FIFTEEN

IN COLIN'S LINE OF WORK, you got to know the ins and outs of police procedure. Who to talk to in order to cut the red tape...how to get your hands on an accident report almost thirty years old. And so it was that Colin sat in the sheriff's office at Silver Lake, reading the report on his father's death.

Thomas's blood alcohol level had been above the legal limit...way above. The accident had been a single-car crash, no one else hurt. Thomas had been driving on a mountain road and had skidded over an embankment. He'd died at the scene, before the paramedics could even get him out of the car.

Slowly Colin set down the report. He needed some air, so he went outside. Alex was sitting on one of the benches that bordered the lawn, waiting for him. She stood as soon as she saw him and joined him as he began walking toward the lakefront. When he didn't speak, she broke the silence.

"Did you find out what you needed to know?"

"Yeah. My father had too much to drink that night—just like a lot of other nights. I guess he was lucky the times he managed to make it home in one piece."

"Colin, I'm sorry."

"Sometimes finding out about the past isn't a relief, is it?"

"No," she said. "It's not."

They'd reached the lake by now. Several boats were out today, and kids splashed along the shore.

"Are you still leaving?" Colin asked.

"Yes. My flight is at one o'clock day after tomorrow."

"Nothing I can do to change your mind?"

"Colin, we've already been through this. I just need some time away from here."

"Away from me," he said.

She stepped out onto the sand, and the breeze ruffled her hair. She looked pretty as usual, but she also looked sad.

"Believe me, I wish it didn't have to be like this. I wish I could just come to you and tell you that everything is all right. But it's not, and I don't know when it will be."

He drew her into his arms anyway. "I don't like you going back to Chicago. It's where your ex-husband is."

He felt her stiffen in his embrace. "I can handle it," she said. "I'm on my guard now."

"Be careful, Alex." He tilted her face toward him. "We have one last night together."

"Colin, if you're thinking about…"

"I'm thinking about it, all right," he said. "But I know it's not likely to happen again. So we'll compromise. You'll have dinner with me tonight."

"I can't do that," she said reluctantly. "A romantic dinner…alone with you…"

"Hardly. I'm inviting you to eat dinner one last time with the McIntyre clan."

She looked ready to say no, but at last she nodded. "One last time," she said softly. And then she kissed him.

ALEX SHOWED UP PROMPTLY at six-thirty for dinner, and learned that Sean was the cook for the evening. She wandered into the kitchen to see if she could help. He was tussling with a large pot of spaghetti. Alex assessed the situation and began stirring the mushroom-and-tomato sauce before it could spatter.

"Damn," Sean said, poking the pasta.

"Next time try rigatoni. Smaller noodles are safer. I learned that the hard way."

"How come you're leaving?" Sean asked.

"Because…because I have to. I have a life back in Chicago, and…"

"Cut the bull," he said.

She almost laughed, even though she wasn't in a jocular mood. "Okay. The truth is, I have a whole lot of questions to deal with, and I have to go somewhere else to find the answers."

"I thought you liked my dad. I thought you liked us."

"I do. Very much. But that's not helping me with the answers. In fact, it's stopping me." She stirred the sauce thoughtfully.

"I wouldn't mind if you stuck around," Sean muttered.

"Right," she said caustically. "So I can run more interference between you and your dad?"

"I can't talk to him." Sean gave the noodles a baleful stare.

"Have you tried?"

"Sure."

"I don't think so," she said. "You're working so hard to take him down a peg or two that you can't possibly have a decent conversation with him."

Now Sean frowned at her. "What the hell does that mean?"

"That you're trying to make your father into somebody less imposing, perhaps. You've built up this larger-than-life image of him, and now you're fighting against it. You McIntyres really are ones for the larger-than-life stuff. Don't you realize everybody's human?''

Sean scowled and didn't seem to have any more to say. Just as well. She wasn't really in a position to offer advice to any of the McIntyres...not with her own life in such a turmoil.

They all sat down to dinner: Herb, Colin, Sean and Alex. And Dusty, of course. The little terrier settled at her feet. She realized again how much she was going to miss them all, no matter how difficult they were.

The three McIntyre males were exceptionally quiet this evening, during dinner and after. None of them responded well to her efforts at conversation. Alex gazed across the table at Colin. He seemed lost in his own thoughts.

''My turn to clean up,'' Herbie said at last.

''I read the police report today,'' said Colin.

''Uh-oh,'' muttered Sean. ''Here we go again.''

''What police report?'' asked Herbie.

''The one that says Thomas died legally intoxicated.''

For a moment there was complete silence around the table. And then Herbie thumped his hand down.

''I told you, I won't hear that anymore—''

"The police report isn't lying. But it can't tell me the whole truth. And that's what I need right now."

Alex looked at Colin once more, and she saw the pain tightening his expression. She understood it all too well. She knew what it was like to need the truth...even when the truth was a terrible thing.

"I won't talk about it," Herbie said.

His face was ashen, and Alex saw his pain, too.

"Dammit, Herb, we have to talk," Colin said.

"Not in front of the boy," said Herb.

"Why not?" Colin asked. "We have too many damn secrets in this family."

"Alex is a shrink," said Sean. "She can give you guys a counseling session, and maybe you'll finally be done with all this crap."

Everyone stared at Sean. Alex shook her head. "I don't think this is the right place or the right time—"

"I'll agree to it," Colin said. "What about you, Herb?"

"I don't need any damn counseling session."

"Maybe you do," Colin said. "Maybe we all do. Something's got to give."

Now everybody stared at Alex. She had experience in family interventions, but never like this. The sessions took place in her office under controlled conditions—not around the dinner table, for goodness' sake.

Then again…Alex was already in too deep, and she knew it. She might as well make this impromptu ''session'' work as well as she could. ''Look, if we're going to do this, all three of you have to be honest. And you might have to accept things that you don't want to hear.''

''Agreed,'' said Colin.

Sean shrugged.

And Herbie, at last, said gruffly, ''I'll listen. That's about all I can promise.''

''I won't be doing the talking,'' she warned him. ''This is between the three of you. Herbie, it's your turn first. Just say what's on your mind—but don't accuse anybody. Especially not Colin.''

That last part seemed to throw him. He placed both hands on the table.

''I want Colin to—all right, all right. I just want…'' He dropped his voice. ''I just want to remember Thomas the way he deserves to be remembered. I don't want to lose the son I had.''

There was a silence, and then Alex turned to Colin. ''You're next. And remember…no accusations.''

''I'd just like to know my father the way he really was. A hero, but a person, too.'' His voice was quiet.

"You call him a drunk, and he'll never be a hero again—"

"Herbie," said Alex. "It's Sean's turn."

"I'm not part of this."

"Yes, you are."

"I want everybody just to leave me alone," he muttered.

"Not good enough."

"I want...I want everybody to stop acting like I'm the one who'll make up for Thomas!"

There was another heavy silence around the table. And then Colin spoke.

"I haven't done that, son."

"Neither have I," said Herb.

Sean frowned at his great-grandfather. "Like hell you haven't. Every time you talk to me, it's like I'm supposed to be *him*. I'm supposed to look like him and sound like him." Now Sean swiveled toward his father. "And you act like I have to be the perfect son because your dad died. So every damn thing we do together has to be *perfect*. And I'm supposed to be perfect. And I'm sick of trying to be perfect. I'm sick of the whole damn perfect thing!"

Sometimes, Alex reflected, counseling sessions actually did their job.

COLIN LAID THEM OUT one at a time: three credit cards, a bank card, some miscellaneous twenties and a fifty. Sean scooped them up and jammed them into his wallet.

"It's about time," he said.

"I still think you want to be a normal kid," Colin told him. "With a normal allowance. But Alex had a point. You've earned your money. It's yours."

A lot had been said last night, a lot that had supposedly cleared the air. So why did he still feel the same old distance between his son and him?

Alex had warned him about this. She'd said that last night was only a beginning, that the McIntyres had a whole lot more to work through. She'd said that when you first ripped the bandage off a wound, it hurt even worse.

He wasn't too sure about the metaphor, but he was beginning to see her point. He'd have to say that this morning Sean seemed more resentful than ever.

"Got any plans today?" Colin asked.

"No." He started scuffing his way toward the door.

"Sean…"

"Yeah?"

The belligerence, all over again.

"Believe it or not, you don't have to be a TV star."

"I'm not a star," Sean muttered.

"Okay, a TV actor—whatever. You could spend a lot more time with me, here in Idaho. This is where I'm going to live from now on. And you could do the community theater thing if you need to go on being...an actor."

"Gee, thanks, Dad," Sean said sarcastically.

"Maybe that didn't come out right." Colin tried again. "I really do think you're good at what you do, Sean."

"Yeah, right. And I think being fifteen sucks." With that, Sean left.

Colin ran a hand through his hair. None of this was going right.

HERB OPENED THE TRUNK in the attic and took out some letters bound with string. He handed them to Colin. "Here. Your dad wrote them to me from Vietnam. Don't come down and talk to me until you've read every one."

"Herb—"

"I don't want to talk right now," his grandfather said. "Just read them." He disappeared through the trapdoor.

Colin sat down and read the first letter. Then the next one and the next. He took his time, and he was thorough—just as Herb had requested.

A couple of hours went by, and then he was finished. Now certain phrases lingered with him:

"...I lie awake at night, and think how tomorrow I could be dead. But maybe that's not what scares me the most. It's knowing I could really mess things up for the other guys... Tell Colin I'm just doing my job...lie to him and tell him I did it well... Everybody thinks I'm crazy for coming back here again. What am I trying to prove, they ask? Maybe I'm just trying to prove I'm not a coward after all."

Colin sat there for a long while, gazing at his father's letters. Then he tied them with the string, put them back in the trunk and went downstairs to his grandfather.

"THE WAR CHANGED EVERYTHING," said Herb, his voice wooden. "Before that, your dad felt that the world belonged to him. Okay, he drank a little too much as a teenager. But he stopped, just the way I told you he did. It wasn't until he went to Vietnam that the drinking started again. You saw what he wrote. He never stopped being scared. I wrote him back, and I told him it was okay. He'd have to be crazy not to be scared. But I guess he never believed me. He kept asking me to cover for him. 'Don't tell Jessie and Colin I screwed up again. Just don't tell them.' That's what he asked. I did it for him, don't you see? I didn't tell you he was scared, and that he drank to make the fear go away...and that once he almost got his own men killed because of the drinking.''

He and Colin were sitting in the living room, surrounded by all the photographs of Thomas. Colin picked up the one that showed Thomas in his uniform, looking boldly and confidently into the camera. He seemed very young.

"But he was decorated," Colin said. "He *was* heroic."

"Dumb luck, he called it. I couldn't convince him otherwise. And I started to realize something. I'd built him up so much when he was a kid, he got cocky...and when real life hit him, he didn't know how to handle it."

"It wasn't your fault," Colin said.

"Easy words."

Colin hated to see his grandfather like this... shrunken somehow, as if only the legend of Thomas McIntyre had been keeping him vigorous, and now that the legend had been diminished somewhat, Herb was diminished, too.

"It wasn't your fault," Colin repeated, but Herb didn't seem to be listening.

"Dammit, I should have been harder on him from the beginning. The waste of it...surviving that hell in Vietnam, and then he comes back and dies on that mountain. The damn waste of his life. That was the terrible joke on all of us.''

''It's okay to be ticked at him.''

''I'm ticked at myself,'' Herb said. ''All these years…don't you get it, Colin? I've been trying to build up my image, as much as Thomas's. I've been trying to paint myself as the perfect dad who fathered the perfect son.''

''Yeah, well, I know about that.''

Herb gave a bitter, humorless laugh. ''Think we've screwed up Sean, as well?''

''Maybe it's not too late.'' Colin had to know everything. ''Frank Rowland said something about my parents almost getting a divorce. I never heard that part, either.''

''For a while there, it was pretty rough going for them. I think your mom worshiped your dad just like all the rest of us did. And when she married him and found out he wasn't so perfect after all…''

''They patched it up, though,'' Colin said.

''They did. Hit her really hard when he died. She blamed herself, too. That's what your mom and I had in common for a long time. Blaming ourselves for Thomas. I guess that's why neither one of us ever told you the truth. We felt so damn guilty. But then she managed to get on with her life…and I didn't.''

"I don't think you've done such a bad job of it."

Herb looked at him closely. "All this time you've been blaming me for not letting you have memories of a real dad. Suddenly you're going to let me off the hook?"

"Yeah," Colin said. "I think I am."

"Don't do me any favors," Herb grumbled.

And that was a good sign. He almost sounded like his old, brusque self.

THE LAKE HOUSE SEEMED particularly empty that night. Colin walked through the rooms, then stood at one of the bay windows and watched the moon glimmer on the water. This would be his home from now on. He felt good about that much. No matter what Alex said about him being unable to "settle down," he was going to give it a try. Whether Sean would be convinced by the effort— that was another thing. Colin could only hope this change would be good for both of them.

Alex was leaving Idaho tomorrow. She was taking a flight to Boise and then she'd head for Chicago. The thought of it made the house seem emptier than ever.

At last Colin felt he understood a couple of things. When the past shadowed you, it was impossible to start a new life for real. So maybe it wasn't fair of him to ask Alex to start a new one...with him. Not as long as the shadows hung over her.

She'd been in this house with him, though, and the memory of her lingered here. He didn't like thinking of Alex as nothing more than a memory. He went outside and started walking along the lakeshore. But they'd done that together, too. Somehow, in the short time she'd been in Idaho, she'd twined herself into every part of his life. He couldn't imagine her gone.

To hell with fairness. He wanted her with him, however it had to be.

He went out to his Jeep, turned the key in the ignition and floored it back to Sobriety.

CHAPTER SIXTEEN

THEY WERE SHOWING A NEW double feature at The Sunshine. Alex sat through both movies, but she scarcely paid attention to what was happening on the screen. She'd been wrong to think that coming here would provide a distraction.

By the time she emerged from the movie theater, night had long since fallen. She welcomed the darkness...but then she saw Colin, leaning against his Jeep at the curb. Her heartbeat accelerated.

"I guess it wasn't too difficult to find me," she said.

"No. You weren't at Maggie's Diner and you weren't at the soda fountain. Not many other choices left."

She began walking down the street, and Colin fell into step beside her.

"Big plans for your last night in town?" he asked.

"Nothing special. Thought I'd while away the time till midnight, then maybe catch a sighting of the ghost down at the mining museum."

"The hauntings run on schedule these days?" he asked dryly.

"Beats me, but now I understand there's a love story involved. Seems the miner—the one who's a ghost—can't rest because he's searching for the woman he once loved. Her name is Mollie, and she used to be one of the saloon girls—"

"Lord," said Colin.

Alex kept on walking. "I found the story touching myself. If the miner—his name is Ned—ever meets up with Mollie, then the two of them can finally go off together. Or float off together, as the case may be. Maybe it's only a story, but it *is* touching."

"You'd think Herb could have named the ghost something besides Ned."

"What's Herbie got to do with it?" Alex asked.

"Guess," Colin said. "You're liable to catch him running around in a white sheet. Or overalls, last I heard. He's trying for authenticity."

Alex smiled. "What do you know. I'm going to miss Herbie."

"He's going to miss you. We're all going to miss you. And that's why we can't let you go, Alex."

She stopped, not looking at him. They'd reached a deserted corner of Main Street, where the shops had already closed for the night. "Are you the delegation from the McIntyres?"

He took her hand and drew her close. "I'm here to argue my own case."

She closed her eyes for a moment, savoring the nearness of him. It was her last night...her very last. Surely she could allow herself this one indulgence.

"I really have made up my mind, Alex," he told her. "I'm staying in Idaho."

"And you're going to buy Steve's Outfitters?"

"Not exactly," he said. "Tonight my grandfather and I came up with an alternative plan. He thinks I should run for county sheriff next election. He says that with his connections I'm a shoo-in. Of course, his connections don't know that he's the county *ghost*."

Alex gazed at Colin through the moonlight. "Sheriff...hmm. That has a certain Type R ring to it."

"Still feel I'm making a mistake?"

She thought it over. "You know, Colin...being sheriff doesn't sound half-bad for somebody like you. Sure, it might be a little more laid-back than saving lives for a living—but I have a feeling it'll allow you to go on being a rescuer, one way or another. I also have a feeling it won't lack for excitement...or challenge. Yes, I can see it."

He drew her even closer. "Glad you approve, Alex. So we can move on to the next item on the agenda. I want you to marry me."

Now her heart truly pounded. She placed both hands on his chest, trying for at least a little distance. "Wait a minute," she said, dismayed at the way her voice trembled. "I thought you didn't believe in outright marriage proposals. I thought the subject was tabled for the future—"

"I figure the future is now," he murmured. "Our future, Alex. Yours and mine. What do you say?"

"Colin, you can't do this to me."

"The question's simple, Alex. Will you marry me?"

She leaned against him now, because the way he made her feel—weak-kneed, breathless, swept away...frightened—had come over her again. Never in her life had she wanted so much to say yes. Simply, unequivocally, yes.

"No, Colin," she whispered.

"No's not an option on this one," he said, not sounding perturbed in the least. "Your arguments aren't going to stand, Alex. I know them all. Number one, you just got divorced and you're not looking for another involvement right away. Okay, you aren't looking, but these things happen. Number two, you still haven't figured out what happened to you all those years ago. I'll help you to find the truth. Number three—''

"No, Colin." Her voice was firmer this time, and at last she had the fortitude to step away from him. The night air suddenly felt too cool, but she didn't return to the protection of his arms. "You're right—the first reason won't stand. So what if I just got divorced? Jonathan was never worth my love, and you...oh, you definitely are." She hurried on before she could lose what little willpower she had left. "But that's just it, you see. It's because you're worth it that I have to leave right now—and I have to leave on my own. I'm confused and afraid. And you don't deserve either of those feelings."

"Alex," he said, "you can't be afraid of me. Not anymore."

"I know it doesn't make any sense, Colin! But there's something about you...something I don't understand. And it *does* make me afraid. Almost as afraid as I feel in my nightmare. Despite all logic, I'm mixing you up with the horror of my dream...and that's not company you deserve to keep."

He was silent, pacing a little away from her.

"In my heart, my gut...something's wrong," she said miserably. "Something's very wrong! I have to figure out what it is before you and I can have anything together.''

"And what if you never figure it out, Alex?" he asked softly. ''What then?''

"I don't know, Colin.'' She had nothing else to offer him.

He came to her then and kissed her. "Goodbye, Alex,'' he said, and she heard the heavy regret in his voice. Then he turned and walked away, leaving her on the street corner. Leaving her alone…just as she'd asked him to do.

"SO THIS TIME YOU'RE GOING for good.'' Tina Scott watched as Alex brought two suitcases out of her room. "Here, I'll help.'' Tina grabbed one of the bags. "Well, did you break Colin's heart?''

Alex would miss a lot of things about Sobriety, Idaho. One of them would be Tina's refreshing, if startling, straightforwardness.

"I think he'll survive," Alex said.

"Honey, I have a philosophy about men like Colin McIntyre. It takes a lot for them to fall, but when they finally do, watch out. Because they fall for good.''

Alex felt that ache deep inside, but she didn't say anything. She and Tina went outside to her rental car. Alex opened the trunk, and Tina tossed the suitcase inside. Alex put the other one next to it.

"Thanks," she said.

"Got everything?"

"Looks like it. Guess you're glad to be seeing the last of me."

Tina shrugged good-naturedly. "It's like I told you. Competition is invigorating. And now…well, I have a feeling that Colin is going to be a little downhearted. He'll need some consoling." She gave her usual dazzling smile.

Alex knew without a doubt that beautiful women would always flock to Colin. If he did need consoling, Tina wouldn't be the only contender. He'd have lots of choices.

She didn't like the stab of jealousy she felt. But she had no right to complain after turning him down.

She slammed the trunk lid with more force than necessary. Then she went to the driver's side and climbed in.

"Goodbye, Tina," she said.

Tina leaned over to peer through the window. "Listen, Alex, for what it's worth, you're letting go of a really great guy."

"I know." She put the car into gear, backed out of the driveway and headed down the street. True, only a few blocks later she had to pull over, blink furiously and wait for the tears to subside.

But then she continued on her way.

SEAN'S NEWEST REBELLION came in the form of the sixteen-year-old girlfriend who arrived by plane from California. Sean had paid her airfare, then hired a limo to transport her from Silver Lake to Sobriety. Of all the accoutrements of stardom, Sean seemed to like limousines the best.

This sixteen-year-old was now standing in the middle of Herb's living room. Her name was Cindy, and she looked way too old for Colin's son.

"Nice to meet you, Cindy," said Herb, apparently deciding to play the understanding great-grandfather. "Guess you'll be staying with us?"

Cindy tore her gaze away from Sean long enough to give a distracted nod.

"Come on, then—we'll find a room for you. This is a big old place."

Herb started up the stairs. Cindy, after a last look at Sean, followed. She wore too-high heels and almost tripped as she went. Her face turned red, and Colin felt sorry for her. He did not, however, feel sorry for his son. As soon as the two of them were alone, he let Sean have it.

"What the hell is this about?"

"Nothing," said Sean. "She's my girlfriend. Now I can't have a girlfriend?"

"You never mentioned her before," Colin said.

"You never asked."

Colin told himself to take it easy. That was what Alex would probably advise him. She'd said that he had a tendency to overreact with Sean—and that only made Sean overreact in turn. But Alex wasn't here. She'd left for Chicago earlier today, and he didn't know when he'd see her again...if ever.

"Okay, I'm asking now," he said. "Why did you fly your girlfriend all the way out here without discussing it with me first?"

Sean folded his arms and stared back at him defiantly. "Would you have said yes?"

"No."

"That's why."

The girl was here and they had to deal with it. "Do her parents know where she is?"

"Sure."

Colin wasn't convinced. "Give me their phone number."

"I don't have it," Sean muttered.

"She's your girlfriend and you don't know her phone number?"

"She doesn't live with her parents," Sean said. "She had a fight with them and now she lives with her aunt."

"Okay," Colin said, with more patience than he felt, "what's the aunt's phone number?"

"Get off my back, Dad. Herbie's being okay about this."

Were Herb and Sean going to be "buddies" again? That didn't bode well.

"Give me the phone number," Colin repeated. Sean mumbled it, then stalked off. Colin dialed California and spoke to a woman who sounded too young to be anybody's aunt. Yes, she knew all about Cindy's visit to Idaho. Yes, she was thrilled that Cindy was spending her vacation with *the* Sean McIntyre.

Colin hung up, less than satisfied. As far as he was concerned, Cindy was going back to California on the next flight out.

Take it easy, a voice in his head said. The voice sounded remarkably like Alex's. She'd probably sit down with the boy and find out what was really going on with him. Too bad she wasn't here.

Who was he kidding? There was really only one reason he missed her. He loved her. And her not being here was why he felt so lousy inside.

THE KID HAD DONE IT AGAIN. He'd run off. And this time he'd taken the girl with him. Sixteen-year-old Cindy in her too-high heels.

Colin could picture all kinds of scenarios, none

of them pleasant. Take two teenagers, add some overactive hormones...no, definitely not pleasant.

He looked everywhere for them. By the time he'd scoured the entire town it was early evening. He'd ended up at Maggie's Diner.

"Haven't seen Sean," Denise said as she brought him a cup of coffee. "And what does this girl look like?"

"Too young for her own good. Too old for Sean."

"That's real helpful," Denise said. "But your boy has the McIntyre genes. From here on, the girls will be swarming around. Too young, too old—you name it."

"Are you trying to make me feel better or worse?"

She swiped the tabletop with her rag. "Just remember what *you* were like as a teenager."

Exactly what he didn't want to recall. "Guess I'll have to drive into Silver Lake, take a look around there."

"Before you do that, what about his performance tonight? Sean's very conscientious and he hasn't missed one yet. He's bound to show up—girlfriend or not."

The Wild West melodrama. Colin had almost forgotten. But it was true; Sean took his small role very seriously. "Thanks, Denise."

"I come through now and then." She swiped the tabletop again, even though it was already perfectly clean. "So, you actually let her get away."

He glanced at Denise sourly. "Got a point?"

"Yes. Even *I* could see the two of you were crazy about each other. What's your problem, Colin?"

He left his coffee half-finished and put his money on the table. "Keep the change, Denise."

"I always do," she said flippantly. "Now, go find your kid."

WHEN SEAN DIDN'T SHOW UP for the performance, Colin headed back to his grandfather's house. He walked all through it, calling his son's name, then Herb's. Where the hell was everybody?

He found a note on the floor next to the coffee table in the living room. Apparently Herb had tossed it onto the table in such haste it had fallen off. It was short and to the point: "Damn kids went into the mine. Going after them."

Colin crumpled the note. A second later he was in the Jeep, flooring it again. And this time he was headed for the mountains.

He made it to the mine entrance in record time, and jolted to a stop next to Herb's old truck. Once he grabbed a flashlight from his glove compartment, he headed down into the mine.

"Herb," he called. Then, "Sean!" His voice echoed, but he heard no other sound. The darkness seemed to have swallowed everyone.

Being a rescue worker, he had honed his instincts over the years, but he hardly needed his instincts now to tell him that something was wrong. He could feel it all through him, just like the cold dampness of the mine.

He went back out to the main entrance and took a large coil of rope from Herb's truck. Then he entered the mine again and anchored the rope to an outcrop. He began traveling the tunnels, one after the other, using the rope always to guide him back to his starting place so he wouldn't get lost. He called Herb's name, Sean's name—over and over. He even called Cindy's name. But the echo of his own voice was his only answer.

A strange clarity came to him in the darkness. He thought back on everything Sean had said or done these past few weeks, and saw the pattern more distinctly than ever: his son trying so desperately to prove his worth against the McIntyre legacy. The defiance, the spending, the running away—all attempts by Sean to stand apart from his family, to be someone on his own. Yet all the while, the kid had been feeling like a failure.

Then Sean had brought his girlfriend to town, no doubt in one more effort to prove his independence. But having to prove himself to the girl, not just to Herb and Colin, could only have increased the pressure. Maybe that was why he'd brought her down into the mine. To show her his bravery. To show her he wasn't afraid of anything...

Wasn't that what Thomas had tried to prove all those years ago in Vietnam? That he could defeat his fears, could measure up after all. He'd had his own impossible image to live up to: golden son of Herb McIntyre, local hero of Sobriety, Idaho. The McIntyres had a too-long history of trying to be perfect.

Systematically, relentlessly, Colin kept on. One tunnel at a time...backtracking, starting down another. Calling out until his voice was hoarse. And then, at last, finding an answer. A terrible answer.

One of the tunnels was blocked floor to ceiling by a tumble of rock. A cave-in, apparently fresh, the air still thick with unsettled dust. He stared at the wall of rock, and the cold in the mine chilled him to the bone.

Now he knew why Herb and Sean hadn't responded.

IT WAS LATE WHEN ALEX pulled over at an all-night diner in Billings. She went in, ordered a cup of tea, and decided the place didn't have nearly the charm of Maggie's Diner. Already she missed Sobriety…everything and everyone in it.

She sipped her tea, knowing she was only a short drive now to her hometown. Thinking back, she couldn't say exactly when she'd decided not to catch that plane in Silver Lake. All she knew was that shortly she'd found herself in her rental car heading toward Montana.

A calm she hadn't known in quite some time had taken her over. She felt she had started down an inevitable path. There would be no more hiding. Not for her—and not for her mother.

She hadn't eaten dinner, so now she ordered some minestrone and crackers. When she finished, she lingered over another cup of tea. Perhaps she was delaying a little, but it didn't matter. She'd be getting on the road again soon.

The end of the journey was near.

SEVERAL LANTERNS FLOODED the mine with light. A crew armed with pickaxes and shovels had started carving away at the barrier of rock, but the going was slow. They couldn't use power tools, for fear of bringing more rock crashing down. Colin worked the hardest. He'd been at it for hours, but he paid no attention to the strain in his muscles.

Jake Morgan, town mining expert, came up beside him. "Take a break, Colin. I've got a whole line of folks out there ready to pitch in."

Colin didn't even listen. "Tell me there's a faster way," was all he said.

"There're faster ways, all right. But they're all dangerous. This tunnel's been an accident waiting to happen. Look at the fracture along there." Jake panned his flashlight over the ceiling. "We're taking enough risks as it is. We could be buried in here, too."

That wasn't one of Colin's worries. He raised his pickax, brought it down again. They had a long way to go. The wall of rock must be very thick if no sound was getting through. He pictured Sean and Herb and the girl calling for help, and their cries ending in nothing but silence. The image was an ugly one, but it was a lot better than the alternative—the three of them making no sound at all...

The coldness invaded Colin all over again, but he kept on. He could sense Jake Morgan gazing at him, could sense the man's pity.

"We'll find them," Jake said. "Count on it."

He wanted to count on something, but he didn't know what. All he had were his aching muscles and the ax in his hand. Then another image flashed into his mind. He remembered the day he and Alex had gone up to the mountainside church built so long ago. And Colin knew what the old priest would be doing right now if he were still alive.

Colin had never been much for religion—not the formal kind, anyway. But he started praying. Even as he wielded that ax, he prayed.

CHAPTER SEVENTEEN

ALEX WAS STAYING AT THE same hotel she and Colin had used on their visit to Penrose. She hadn't expected to sleep, but at some point she finally drifted off. As usual, the nightmare came again, like an old enemy long familiar now. The fire...the looming presence she suspected was her father. Shaking her, hurting her...

She woke up trembling, bathed in sweat, the noon sunlight oddly harsh as it streamed through the window. She couldn't believe she'd slept this long. Hurriedly she showered and dressed. Lunch was nothing more than a doughnut grabbed in the hotel lobby.

But what was she hurrying for, anyway? Her mother wouldn't get home from work for several hours yet. Feeling keyed up and let down at the same time, Alex drove aimlessly around town, hardly noticing her surroundings.

At last her body demanded more sustenance. She went into a fast-food place and got the bare minimum—a burger, some fries and an orange soda. She ate without tasting her food, then went back to the car. Once again she drove aimlessly. But then she knew she really had nowhere else to go. She headed for her mother's house, got out of the car and sat down on the porch steps to wait.

TEARS STREAKED LILLIAN'S face as she carried a shovelful of rubble to one of the wheelbarrows. She wore a hard hat that perched precariously on top of her head. She said that Herb had always insisted on hard hats for anybody who went into the mine, and she wasn't about to go against him now. She'd already repeated this bit of information to Colin several times—as if, by obeying Herb's rules, she would be able to get him out safely.

"Take a rest," Colin told her. "You're working too hard."

"What if I told you the same thing?" she shot back. And then, "Oh, I'm sorry, Colin. But I want to see him again. That's all I want. Just to see him again. And I don't give a damn who finds out about us. I'll take out an ad...I'll put up announcements. I'll let everybody know that I'm seeing Herbie McIntyre." She swiveled toward Tina Scott, who was approaching with a tray of coffee cups. "Do you hear?" she said defiantly. "I'm in love with that old coot Herbie."

"You don't need to tell *me,*" Tina said. "I knew about you two a long time ago."

Lillian stared at her, as if grateful for any distraction. "How did you know?"

"You dropped enough hints. The way you purposely changed the subject whenever his name was mentioned, the way you kept that secret little smile. A dozen other clues. Give me *some* credit for knowing about men and women. And if Herbie thinks *he's* so good at being devious…when you haul him out of this place, tell him to stop running around town in that sheet of his."

"You know about that, too?" Lillian asked faintly.

"Honey, I figured it out the first time Rose Bradshaw had a sighting at the mining museum. Like I said—give me *some* credit."

Tina came over to Colin and handed him some coffee. "I'm so sorry about all this. You can't imagine how sorry."

For once, Tina Scott wasn't trying to flirt with him. She just seemed to be offering her support, the way the rest of the town was doing. So many people had gathered here, working in shifts, giving whatever they could. But almost twenty-four hours had gone by and still they hadn't made nearly enough of a dent in that wall of rock. And still they hadn't heard a sound from Sean or Herb.

Colin had known fear before. In his line of work, he'd have to be crazy not to experience a healthy dose of trepidation now and then. Sometimes it was all that kept him in one piece. But he'd never known anything like this—the gut-wrenching fear that he'd never see his son or his grandfather alive again.

GAYLE WAS LATE GETTING home from work. Perhaps she'd sensed somehow that her daughter had returned, and she'd wanted to avoid Alex. But here she was at last, coming slowly up the walk.

"Hello, Alex," she said. "I expected you back. Perhaps not quite this soon...but I did expect you."

They went into the house together, and Gayle put on the kettle. For the first time, Alex allowed herself to see this similarity between her mother and her: they both preferred tea to coffee. A few minutes later they sat down at the dining room table, a cup in front of each of them.

"I know you want to hear more about your father," Gayle said.

Alex nodded, not saying anything.

"I've been thinking about what to tell you. I suppose I always knew there'd come a time when you'd ask about him. But I can't tell you how grateful I was for your lack of curiosity while you were growing up.''

Alex wrapped both hands around her cup. "Didn't it seem strange to you that I *wasn't* more curious?"

Her mother's gaze flickered away. "No. I just saw it as a blessing. All I could do was hope that you'd forgotten about…about the times he'd hurt us. And when it seemed that you *had* forgotten, I could only be grateful."

"I didn't forget completely," Alex said softly. "Things are coming back little by little. But it's agonizing, Mom."

Gayle raised her cup, then set it down again without drinking. "He was very charming in the beginning." She spoke without expression. "I fell in love almost the first moment I saw him. He promised me so much…promised to make everything better. I've never told you this, Alex, but my parents were…difficult people."

"Abusive?" Alex had to ask, wondering how far back the history went.

But Gayle shook her head. "No, not that bad. They just didn't appear to care about me very much. Both of them almost seemed relieved when I got married and moved away."

This struck an uncomfortable chord. When Alex had gone off to Chicago for college, her mother had seemed relieved to see her go. Maybe you just kept repeating your parents' mistakes.

Gayle had stopped speaking, and Alex had to prod her.

"Go on. We can't stop now."

Gayle studied her. "Are you here to judge me?" she asked in a strangely hollow voice.

"No. I just want the truth, that's all."

"You *think* you want the truth." At last Gayle showed a flash of spirit. "Well, here it is—let's see if you can take it. The beatings started almost as soon as I married your father. I couldn't go back to my parents—not when they didn't want me. And I didn't know how to leave him. He said…he always said he'd kill me if I left. And I believed him. Why shouldn't I have believed him?"

Alex gave no argument. She meant what she'd said—she hadn't come here to judge.

"I tried to understand why he was like that," Gayle said, clenching her hands. "Why did he look for any excuse to hurt me—*why?* When I couldn't find the answer in him, I thought maybe it was me. I thought maybe I would bring out that contempt, that anger, in any man. I really did think it. Until you came along, and eventually he started hurting you, too. And then I just didn't care any more *why* it was happening. I only wanted it to stop."

Alex reached across the table, tried to take her mother's hand. Gayle shook her head.

"Let me finish. I let it go on too long, Alex. I knew I had to end it, but I didn't know how. And then, finally…I had the strength. I took you and ran away, in spite of all his threats. We didn't have any money, didn't have any place to go, but we went anyway. And then it was almost as if justice was served. Only a few weeks after we left, he died of a heart attack. I tried to mourn him, but I couldn't. All I knew was that you and I were free—and he could never hurt either one of us again."

Alex closed her eyes briefly. It all sounded too…rehearsed. And it didn't even come close to explaining what was behind her horrible nightmare.

"There was a fire, Mom. I know there was."

After a few moments, Gayle's face crumpled, and she began to cry.

Alex realized that she had never seen her mother weep before. Especially not like this—great sobs racked her entire body. Alex pushed her chair back and went around the table to Gayle. She led her to the living room. They both sat down on the couch, and Alex kept her arm around her mother as she continued to weep. They stayed like that for a long while, until at last Gayle had cried herself out. Alex handed her a tissue.

"I never wanted you to know," Gayle said, her voice raw. "It really did seem a blessing when you couldn't remember. I just wanted to protect you, Alex. That's all I ever wanted."

"I believe you," Alex murmured, still holding Gayle. "And I don't blame you. Whatever it is you did...you were in a desperate situation. Who am I to say what anyone should do in a situation like that...."

Gayle straightened a little, turning her head to look at Alex. "What are you thinking?" she whispered. "Do you think I *did* something to him?"

"I don't know what to think, Mom. But if you felt you had no other way out... I'm trying as hard as I can to understand."

Gayle made a garbled sound, and Alex saw that she was crying again, as if all the emotions in her had finally found release.

"Oh, Alex, how could you think...but of course how could you think *otherwise*... No, I didn't kill your father. At times I wanted to, but I never hurt him. You see...hurting was what *he* did. I couldn't be like him."

"I'm glad," Alex said shakily, not knowing until this moment how relieved she would feel. She hung on to her mother. And, after another moment,

Gayle reached out a hand and hesitantly touched Alex's cheek. All these years, she had wanted such a gesture of tenderness and love from her mother…

"He was the one who set the fire," Gayle said at last. "I was cooking dinner, and there was something about it he didn't like. He'd had another bad day at work, and he came into the kitchen and started in on me. He smashed one of the pots on the stove…that's how the fire began. We had this old gas stove that probably should have been condemned, and the fire just flared up. I tried to put it out—but he dragged me away. He shoved me into the bedroom and locked the door. And he stood on the other side and told me I deserved to die." Now Gayle stared straight ahead and pressed her hands together. "I pounded and pounded on the door, but he wouldn't open it. And then I heard you cry, Alex. You were in your room, crying for me."

A shudder went through her, and Alex held her more tightly than before. "It's okay, Mom," she murmured. "I'm okay, I'm safe now, and that's all that matters."

Gayle just went on speaking as if she hadn't heard a word. "He said we were all going to die— you, me and him, too. He almost sounded glad, as if he'd been so miserable for so long he welcomed any escape. Again I pounded and pounded on the door, but he still wouldn't open it. So I went to the window and broke it—and I got out of the house that way. I went back in through the front door so I could get you. The flames were everywhere, and the smoke, but I just kept going. I knew I had to reach you. He'd gone into your room, and he was just standing there, and he was telling you that he was sorry. I grabbed you and I tried to get you away. But then…after that I don't remember. I think I passed out from the smoke. The next thing I knew, both you and I were on the lawn and the firemen were everywhere. They told me he hadn't survived…that he was in the house. That he was dead.''

Alex drew a deep breath. "He got us out, didn't he? And then he went back inside."

"That's what I always assumed. It made him into a sort of hero in the end. Only, I never told anybody that he saved us. I cheated him of that. It was the only revenge I knew for all the suffering he had caused."

"I blocked everything out, didn't I?" Alex murmured. "I was six years old, and I didn't know how to handle what had happened."

"It was a blessing that you forgot," Gayle repeated, her voice suddenly forceful. "I don't care what you tell me—I don't even care if you hate me—I just thanked God that you didn't remember any of it. We moved a short time later. I'd intended to leave Montana far behind. It's funny—I only got two counties away. Believe me, I tried everything I could to give us a fresh start here in Penrose."

"I don't hate you, Mom."

"I never wanted you to know I stayed with a man like that... I never wanted you to know that I allowed him to hurt you. And now that you *do* know—of course you must hate me." Gayle's voice had gone flat.

"No. I don't hate you. I understand."

"How can you, Alex! You would never be as weak as I was. Never..."

"For whatever reasons, Mom, I married a man too much like my father."

Gayle lifted her gaze, searched Alex's face worriedly. "Not Jonathan—he didn't—"

"Almost. I left before it got physical."

"Thank God," Gayle whispered. "Then you *are* stronger than me."

"I married him in the first place, and that's enough to help me understand. Mom, you're exhausted after all this. Here, put your feet up..." Alex got her mother to lie down on the couch. She brought an afghan and smoothed it over her. "Close your eyes for a minute. Just rest for now."

"I'm the one who should be taking care of you. But I've never done a very good job of that, have I?"

Alex smiled just a little. "I'd say it's been just the opposite. The night of the fire, Mom, you went back in for me. You risked your life to save mine. You were the true rescuer that day."

Alex watched as Gayle's eyelids drifted downward. When it seemed that at last her mother slept, Alex moved away from her and went to the window. The sun was setting, tinting the sky in shades of purple and rose—and crimson, the color of fire...

Maybe fire would always be something that frightened her, made her uneasy. But the rest of the fear...it was gone. She believed she understood everything now. When she'd first seen that video of Colin, it had stirred long-suppressed memories. She'd witnessed Colin the rescuer, and mixed him up with the other man who had rescued her as a child—her father. No wonder she'd felt both fascination and terror.

"Will you ever forgive me, Alex?"

Apparently her mother wasn't asleep after all. Alex went back to her and knelt beside the couch. "We'll forgive each other. We've been so distant...and we're both at fault for that. Not just you."

"I felt so guilty," Gayle said. "All these years, I felt guilty for everything that ever happened to you. I just didn't know how to make up for it."

And so Gayle had retreated, reserving her emotions for the artwork she created. Alex picked up the small sculpture from the coffee table, the one that showed a woman dancing. Although it conveyed solitude, the woman's arms were lifted, as if beckoning to someone unseen.

"It's beautiful," she said. "And hopeful."

"Are you saying there's hope for us, Alex?"

She squeezed her mother's hand. "Oh, yes. There's hope."

COLIN'S ARMS WERE BEYOND sore, his throat was clogged with dust and he couldn't remember the last time he'd had anything to eat or to drink. None of it mattered. He just lifted the ax again.

"You have to stop," Denise said. "You can't go on like this."

"We're making headway." It was little enough, but they were carving a passage through the rubble.

"You're going to collapse."

That wouldn't happen, not until he'd reached his son and his grandfather. Denise bent forward with her ax. And then froze.

"Listen!" she exclaimed.

Colin stopped. He heard it, too. A faint cry from the other side of the rubble. Very faint. But still...the sweetest sound Colin had ever heard.

At least one of them was alive. He just kept on praying that all three of them had made it.

ALEX REALIZED THAT IF SHE was going to keep making this trip between Idaho and Montana—and back again—she'd have to get a little more efficient at it, find an easier way to do it. She'd turned her rental car in at Billings, caught a flight to Silver Lake and now she was in another rental car, headed for Sobriety.

She reached Tina Scott's bed-and-breakfast just in time to take advantage of the breakfast part. After hauling her suitcases out of the trunk, she went up the walk and rang the doorbell. *I'm home,* she wanted to call out. Although of course her real home would be with Colin, on the lake...

Tina swung open the door. For once she looked awful, dark shadows under her eyes, her red hair poking in all directions.

"What's wrong?" Alex asked. "What happened to you?"

Several emotions crossed Tina's face at once, but then she shook her head. "Oh, hell," she said. "You'd better go to him."

Alex felt an iciness creep through her. "What are you talking about? What's happened to Colin—"

"It's not him. It's Herbie and Sean and some

girl from California. They're trapped in the mine. A cave-in. Colin's trying to get them out. Everybody's trying.''

"Oh, Lord," Alex said.

Tina snatched up her keys, then grabbed Alex and hauled her out the door. "I'll drive you. He needs you, and since I'm being noble about giving him up, I might as well go all the way."

CHAPTER EIGHTEEN

ALEX FLEW TO COLIN'S ARMS and held on to him for all she was worth. Then, at last, she stepped back and looked at him in the lantern light deep underground. His face was grim, covered in sweat and dirt...much like the first time she'd seen it on that video. But this time she felt no fear. All she knew was her love for him.

"What can I do?" she asked.

"Just be here." His voice was hoarse.

"They're all right. They *have* to be all right."

"We've heard the girl's voice—calling for help, we think. But it was very faint, and we haven't been able to hear anything else since."

"They have to be all right," she repeated. And then, because words were of no use, she just got to work with the rest of them, helping to haul out buckets of rubble. She didn't know how much time passed. She only knew that she would remain at Colin's side, for however long it took.

Eventually someone told her that it was afternoon...then evening. And then someone said it was already midnight…and on they kept, burrowing through the pile of rock.

At last they got a break. They reached a pocket that had not been filled in by rubble, and they managed to move forward several yards. Colin shouted Herb's name, then Sean's, then Cindy's. The girl answered. This time she sounded much closer, and they could actually make out what she was saying.

"Please," she begged over and over. "Please help us…please…"

Colin spoke to her, calmed her down. And gradually they got some answers from her.

"Yes…yes, Sean's okay but he can't talk. He shouted so much that he lost his voice. And Grandpa Herbie, I don't know…he's unconscious…please, please help us…"

That would have to do for now. They worked with renewed energy, Colin and Alex and the rest of them. Surely only a little farther. Surely…

Suddenly a strange rumbling filled the air. The next thing Alex knew, Colin had pressed her to the ground and was crouched over her. Rocks pelted down on both of them, and a stab of pain went up her leg. And now she *was* afraid. She couldn't lose him, not now.

"Colin—are you all right?"

"I'll live," was his terse reply. He pushed several of the rocks aside and helped her up. "We have to get to them and fast, or a whole lot more of us are going to be trapped under here.''

The crew worked feverishly now. It seemed an eternity as they carved their way forward inch by inch. But at last there was just enough of an opening for Colin to squeeze through, then Alex. She swung her flashlight around and saw Herbie stretched out on the ground, face pallid. She saw Sean and Cindy kneeling together, working frantically at the wall of rubble themselves, as if determined to burrow their way out from their side. And then she saw Sean stumble into Colin's arms, saw him burst into a flood of tears and saw Colin rock him as if he were a very young child.

HERB WAS CAUSING TROUBLE at the Silver Lake Hospital. He didn't think he should have to lie in bed this long, and he hated cottage-cheese salad.

''Why can't they ever serve anything decent in this place?''. he grumbled.

Colin pulled a chair up to the side of the bed. ''Just think—when you do get out of here, you might even be glad for Sean's cooking. Or mine.''

''Not likely.'' Herb tried to sit up, winced and sank back down again, rubbing his hand over the bandage on the back of his head. ''Nothing like a mine tunnel collapsing on you. Even a hard hat won't do for that.''

"Sean says you saved him and Cindy—that you pushed them aside just in time."

"Told you—I know that mine. I know when it's time to get out of the way." Herb paused. "Listen, Colin, don't be too hard on the boy. Believe me, I gave him a good talking-to once we were trapped down there. Before I passed out, that is."

"I think he's being hard enough on himself," Colin said. "My suspicion was right. He took Cindy down there to show off. They're lucky you found out about it."

"Just put two and two together," Herb said. "I figured the kid had been talking way too much about the mine. And then when he didn't show up…"

"I just wish you hadn't gone down there alone."

"Did what I had to do…just like you would have done."

Colin couldn't argue with that. "Sean wants to see you, but he thinks you're going to be mad at him."

"He thinks right. But get my great-grandson in here."

A moment later, both Sean and Colin stood beside Herb's bed. Sean made an effort to look bored, but it didn't last. He jammed his hands into his pockets.

"I'm sorry, Grandpa Herbie," he mumbled.

"You told me that already. Next time, just find an easier way to impress a girl, okay?"

Cindy would be flying back to California today; she'd had enough excitement to last her for a very long while. And that meant the three McIntyres would be spending some time alone together, trying to be a family for once. Colin put his hand on his son's shoulder. For a few seconds, he thought maybe Sean would pull away. Old habits, after all, were hard to break. But then Sean glanced at him and stepped just a little closer.

They were going to be all right.

COLIN HELPED ALEX WALK through the lake house. She limped a little. During that second cave-in, a fair-sized rock had struck her just below the knee, although nothing was broken.

The house was still empty, but Alex was telling him again the decorating ideas she had for each room.

"Colin, you're not paying attention," she said, an exasperated look on her face.

"Yes, I am. I'm paying attention to what matters." He put his arms around her and drew her close. He'd been doing this a lot lately, and he never tired of it. She was prettier than ever today, her blond hair falling loose over her shoulders, her brown eyes catching the sparkle of the sun. No more shadows followed her, and that was the best part.

"Are you sure you won't miss Chicago?" he asked.

"Idaho has a way of growing on a person. Besides, here I'll be able to afford an office right next to the lake. It will be very therapeutic for my clients to look out the window and see all that lovely water. Plus I'll be the only shrink for miles. I'm bound to have all the business I can handle."

"You're beautiful," he murmured, kissing her.

She tried to give him a severe look. "You're distracting, Colin. We have so much planning to do. Our wedding, for example. If we don't get going, Herbie and Lillian will beat us to the altar."

He kissed her again, a long and leisurely kiss. "We have another reason to hurry up the wedding. Herb may be giving you away, but Sean's going to be the best man. We want it to happen before he goes back to California."

She laced her fingers behind his neck, gazing at him. "Guess you're disappointed to know your son's still going to be a TV star."

Colin smiled a little. "If you want to know the truth, I wouldn't mind them canceling the damn series. Deep down, I don't think Sean would mind it, either. There are a lot of things he wants to do with his life, and acting's only one of them. Meanwhile, he wants to fulfill his responsibilities. We just have to make sure they don't get him down.'' Now his smile broadened. "A shrink in the family should come in handy.''

"Joining the family's convenient for me, too,'' she said in mock seriousness. "Being married to a rescuer will do wonders for my research. I'll have firsthand knowledge of the Type R male.''

"Not that again,'' he groaned.

"But right now I have other research in mind. Are you game?''

He drew her closer yet. She was right where she was supposed to be—in his arms. "Always,'' he said.

She smiled back at him. "Always and forever, my love.''

HARLEQUIN®
SUPERROMANCE®

Three childhood friends dreamed of becoming
firefighters. Now they're members of the same team
and every day they put their lives on the line.

They are

An exciting new trilogy by

Kathryn Shay

#871 FEEL THE HEAT
(November 1999)
#877 THE MAN WHO LOVED CHRISTMAS
(December 1999)
#882 CODE OF HONOR
(January 2000)

Available wherever Harlequin books are sold.

HARLEQUIN®
Makes any time special ™

 **HARLEQUIN®**
Makes any time special ™

 WIN A DREAM

In celebration of Harlequin®'s golden anniversary

Enter to win a *dream!* You could win:

- A luxurious trip for two to *The Renaissance Cottonwoods Resort* in Scottsdale, Arizona, or

- A bouquet of flowers once a week for a year from **FTD**, or

- A $500 shopping spree, or

- A fabulous bath & body gift basket, including **K-tel**'s *Candlelight and Romance* 5-CD set.

Look for **WIN A DREAM** flash on specially marked Harlequin® titles by Penny Jordan, Dallas Schulze, Anne Stuart and Kristine Rolofson in October 1999*.

FTD

RENAISSANCE.
COTTONWOODS RESORT
SCOTTSDALE, ARIZONA

K·TEL

"This book is DYNAMITE!"
—**Kristine Rolofson**

"A riveting page turner..."
—**Joan Elliott Pickart**

"Enough twists and turns to keep everyone
guessing... What a ride!"
—**Jule McBride**

See what all your favorite authors
are talking about.

Coming October 1999 to a retail store near you.

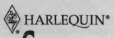
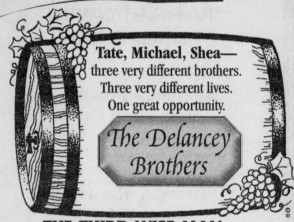